PAULINE TAIT is a novelist and
writing in Perthshire, Scotland. Af
tical Technician for just over twen
Literacy Support, Pauline is now w

Pauline's years of experience in working with and assessing
children from Primaries one to seven, who needed extra-
curricular support, then creating and delivering individual
learning plans to meet their specific needs, has only fuelled
her passion to encourage our younger generations in their own
reading and writing. And this passion has influenced both the
writing and production processes of her picture books. The
covers are tactile, while care is given to the internal layouts to
ensure they engage and inspire.

Pauline also writes Romantic Suspense where care is
given to the credibility of her characters and their emotions.
It is essential to Pauline that emotions and reactions are true
to her chosen topics while the landscape and settings are truly
authentic to their locations.

Sign up for news and mailings at www.paulinetait.com.

Also by Pauline Tait

Novels
A Life of Their Own

Children's Books
The Fairy in the Kettle
The Fairy in the Kettle's Christmas Wish
The Fairy in the Kettle Gets Magical

Abigail Returns

Pauline Tait

For Sharon

Thank you for taking the time to read Abigail Returns!

P. Tait

a

FOUNTAINBRIDGE
PUBLISHING

Published in 2023 by Fountainbridge Publishing

Text copyright © Pauline Tait 2023

ISBN 978-1-7392443-0-9 (paperback)
Also available as an ebook

Page design and typesetting by SilverWood Books
www.silverwoodbooks.co.uk

For my aunt Elizabeth Dunn
April 1945 – April 2022

Acknowledgements

I am extremely grateful to the team I have managed to build around my writing career, many of whom, I'm delighted to say, have become friends in my personal life too.

To PC Sean Robertson for giving your time and allowing me to interview you. My first interview over a cooked Scottish breakfast.

To fellow author and retired GP, Jacqueline James for answering my medical questions.

To fellow author Lis McDermott for reading through my completed manuscript and for being you!

To Isabelle Knight, PR & Marketing expert, for your invaluable expertise and for always being there.

To my editor, Claire Cronshaw.

To my author friends who, although haven't played a direct

part in the publication of this book, have become forever a part of my life, and make the writing community such a fun and friendly place to be.

And to my husband and children who make my world a better place.

Chapter One

An inquisitive glance from a fellow passenger was enough to reassure Abigail. Now, at least, if things were to get out of hand, Abigail knew she wasn't alone. Adjusting the rolled-up coat she'd wedged against the train's rattling window, she attempted to drown out the escalating differences of opinion currently unravelling between her two unwanted seating companions.

For the last twenty or so miles, she'd had no option but to listen as the Impeccably Dressed Italian had become more animated during his heated conversation with the American Tourist. And as he stroppily rose from his seat, he bid his temporary neighbour a bad-tempered *Arrivederci* before disappearing into the other carriage. Abigail couldn't help but replay the recent events in her head, all the while ensuring she turned another page in her novel.

She was hoping she'd given his American adversary, still seated beside her, the illusion that she'd been far too engrossed in the world of Agatha Christie to have noticed for one second what had just taken place at the cosy little table for four. A table they'd supposedly arrived at by chance.

But Abigail knew exactly why they'd chosen to sit beside her. Her tear-stained face, her red swollen eyes that ached from hours of sobbing, and the fact she still wore the stuffy tweed theatre costume she'd worn yesterday – the one that'd unfortunately come with a wig of tousled curls.

Dressed in an outfit more suited to someone fifty years her senior, and surrounded by an array of mismatched luggage, Abigail felt as though her life had been whipped from beneath her once again.

She barely recognised the person she'd become, or the tumultuous twist her life had taken in only a few short hours.

And for the second time in her twenty-nine short years, Abigail found herself mourning a life she'd once known. A life she'd fought so desperately hard to create after fleeing the Scottish island for the city lights only six years before.

Old cases, storage boxes, and shopping bags – all of which would've been out of date in her mother's youth – gave the impression that Abigail was an innocent, naive non-traveller, who was more out of place on the train than her unwanted travelling companions. A sure bet for two dodgy characters with a shady deal to conclude. But, as they say, never judge a book by its cover.

*

As the antics of Agatha Christie's characters began to blur, Abigail's drooping eyelids meant she had no option but to abandon her novel, even if it did mean leaving herself open to unwanted conversation with the American Tourist.

And after attempting, but failing, to stretch life into her waning limbs by clasping her outstretched hands, Abigail's stifled yawns broke into a spasmodic rapture, causing her eyes to water and her nose, not yet recovered from her hours of sobbing, to stream.

In a desperate attempt to compose herself and stay awake, Abigail turned her attention to the passing countryside.

Delivery vans and lorries – such constants as the train had hurried them north from London, through the English countryside and into the Scottish Borders – had become sparse as they'd meandered their way through the Highlands towards the west coast.

Villages had become scattered, and the distant flickers of light served only to remind Abigail of just how remote and sparsely populated the enchanting landscape was.

But there was no excitement at the thought of her journey coming to its end. Instead, she could only sit, trapped between a world she felt removed from and a fellow traveller who'd caused the hairs on the back of her neck to shiver the moment he'd entered the carriage.

And still struggling to process the events of the last forty-eight hours, Abigail's hand skirted her cheek as she wiped at yet another silent tear.

She'd always known that turbulent emotions were bound

to accompany her as she made the dreaded journey back to Lochside, to a life she could barely remember and a house she hated. But the train, zigzagging its way through the disinterested countryside, only served to emphasise her disconnection from the life she'd once known.

And, as if the universe had been listening in on her thoughts, screeching brakes reduced the train to a trundle. They were approaching her stop. Coincidentally, the end of the line.

Closing her eyes, Abigail took a deep breath, as though these actions alone would give her the courage to begin the final leg of her journey.

The brakes brought the train to a stop just as Abigail was opening her eyes. Twelve and a half hours after leaving a rain-soaked London, she'd arrived in the tiny village of Kyle of Lochalsh, on the west coast of Scotland.

Floating burnt oranges and golds danced above her. The late April sun ensuring it went down in style did little to lift Abigail's spirits.

But from somewhere, in the depth of her being, she found the strength to force herself to her feet. Whatever was in store for her at Lochside was far less intimidating than her current seating companion.

She thanked the American Tourist as he stood, allowing her to escape her window seat and the mysterious microcosm that'd been her world for the final miles of her journey. Abigail began to gather her luggage, all the while sensing her seating companion was just as reluctant as she was to make eye contact.

What was it about this man that unnerved her so? What

was it that caused her skin to shiver at the mere sight of him? And why had the sound of his voice caused her stomach to lurch and cramp like knots tightening in a vice?

She racked her brains. But like everything else, if it wasn't a memory from the first decade of her life, or the previous six years, then it was trapped in a dark void she was incapable of unlocking.

While edging her way towards the door, Abigail noticed the American Tourist had retaken his seat, picked up a newspaper, and was resting his feet on the seat opposite.

The writer in her was ever curious: odd that his journey wasn't over, given they'd reached the end of the line…

He was still occupying Abigail's thoughts as she fought to unload her luggage. There had been no lids for the storage boxes, and the shopping bags were reluctant to stay upright. A man in his sixties, who disembarked alongside her, came to her aid with a trolley. His charcoal-grey walking trousers and pristine white T-shirt screamed *tourist*. 'Thank you,' she managed, before continuing to play Jenga with her belongings for what seemed an eternity.

By the time she'd secured her luggage, the travellers who'd exited the train with Abigail had long gone, leaving her alone. The quaint country platform that skirted the shoreline was eerily quiet, apart from a local dog walker who appeared to be admiring Loch Alsh, the sea inlet that was currently separating her from her destination.

Pausing a minute to catch her breath, Abigail allowed herself to take in her surroundings.

The Isle of Skye, her reluctant destination, lay tauntingly close. Though just across the water, it felt as if it was within touching distance when compared to the miles she'd travelled since leaving Kings Cross.

Memories of her early childhood surged to the fore. Reminding her, once again, of where she was and why she'd returned. And as she looked out over Loch Alsh, her gaze was transfixed on the familiar hills that reached beyond the small village of Kyleakin.

But the stark contrast to the city was nothing compared to the clean, crisp sea air that'd engulfed her nostrils the moment she'd stepped from the train.

Abigail's grip on the trolley tightened. Taking a deep breath, she filled her lungs with what her grandmother had called *the purest air on the planet*. Exhaling slowly, Abigail mustered the courage to begin the final leg of her journey.

With her trolley's contents shaking precariously, Abigail guided her luggage towards the taxi rank. A flash of despondency surged at the realisation that all her worldly possessions could be heaped onto a railway station trolley. But she had become a pro at brushing aside her emotions and she quashed her despair, though just in the nick of time.

A sliver of reflective glass caught her eye, causing her hand to reach down and tug at the stuffy theatre costume.

Her skirt was so loose it'd worked its way around and was now sitting back-to-front. The matching padded jacket gave her a rotundness that was out of proportion with the rest of her body. And, as she continued to examine her caricature, she noticed how her slim legs appeared to awkwardly support her padded frame. Plus, as if to add insult to injury, her make-up which, as instructed, had been layered on thick, only served to emphasise her tear-stained face.

Far too exhausted to begin sorting herself out, Abigail turned her back on her reflection. She decided instead, given recent events, that her appearance was the least of her worries.

Instead, she focussed on hauling her unruly trolley towards the small taxi rank just in time to see the American Tourist standing first in line. She strained to listen as he gave his destination, but his words were drowned out when two locals greeted each other from either side of the street. The American Tourist's destination remained a mystery.

Pondering the strange encounter between the American Tourist and the Italian businessman, Abigail steadied the trolley while a driver struggled to cram her luggage into his taxi.

She'd no idea what shady deal had just taken place between the two unlikely acquaintances, but the curious streak in her meant it was still preying on her mind. After all, why had the American Tourist been so eager to give the impression he would not be disembarking at her stop?

'Excuse me, madam,' her driver interrupted. 'Your destination?' His exasperated tone alluded to the fact that this wasn't the first time he'd asked the all-important question.

Remembering her hideous ensemble, she discarded her offence at his use of the word *madam* and gave her destination. 'Lochside, south of Dunvegan, please.' But just as Abigail was about to step into the taxi, she returned her attention to the driver. 'There's a crooked sign at the roadside, near the old lodge. It's white, I think.'

Astonished, Abigail took her seat. Where on earth had that snippet of information come from?

The inexplicable fear Abigail had felt at the sight of the American Tourist was now replaced by trepidation. Aware she was sitting bolt upright, she fought to relax and calm her breathing. The taxi made its way across the Skye road bridge, a feat of engineering more used to transporting excited tourists from the mainland to the peace and tranquillity of the picturesque Isle of Skye.

But Abigail was no tourist. She was grappling memories from her childhood. Memories that seemed determined to flood her thoughts with each passing mile.

Yet so much had changed. And as she watched the miles roll by, she combed the landscape for anything familiar.

But she'd lost a decade to dissociative amnesia. Were these new buildings? She remembered the landscape as barren, not sporadically dappled with these structures. Familiar farms and crofts had either been abandoned, converted into homes and holiday homes, or expanded with shiny new sheds and machinery.

As they travelled further north to Sligachan, then west towards Dunvegan, Abigail reflected on how many of the old country roads had been widened, no longer single tracks with passing places.

Abigail found herself feeling saddened by the changes but couldn't quite understand why. After all, she loathed the place.

Eventually, they reached the old lodge. It looked abandoned and more dilapidated than Abigail remembered. And just as she'd predicted, her driver turned off to the left, onto one of the single-track roads Abigail had been reminiscing about earlier.

He followed it as it hugged the rugged landscape leading to the shore. They snaked through a contrasting mix of rogue birch, oak, and beech trees that'd somehow survived in their battle against the North Atlantic winds, the occasional sliver of plantation woodland, and the vast barren land that'd been given over to sheep long before Abigail's late grandmother had claimed her little patch.

Abigail could only watch as she was whisked along the dirt track she'd cycled along so often as a child. Once again, her memories leaped to the fore. Memories she'd blotted out. Memories she wasn't too keen to have brought to the surface.

It frustrated her that the only years she could remember were filled with loneliness and abandonment. But at the same time, she feared her lost years protected her from far worse.

'It's certainly remote out here.'

'Yeah.' Abigail groaned. 'That was always the problem.'

The driver squinted at her in his mirror, but to Abigail's relief, he continued their journey in silence. His focus was now on more pressing matters, such as dodging potholes and fallen branches that lay scattered before them in the fading light. It reminded Abigail of a children's puzzle, finding their way through the maze to the pot of gold at the end of the rainbow.

But there was no getting away from the fact that each dodged pothole and fallen branch was taking her closer to

17

Lochside, and closer to the life she'd fled six years before.

An ache formed in the pit of her stomach. Nervous jitters spread through her limbs, causing her body to tremble. And she was suddenly aware of her breathing, almost feeling the need to remind herself when to inhale and when to exhale.

But it was the taxi coming to a halt and the driver announcing his fee that finally pulled Abigail from her thoughts.

'What the f—' Abigail screeched, cupping her face in her hands. She peered tentatively between her fingers, as though that would in some way reverse the mess that lay before her.

Her driver was having quite the opposite reaction. Unable to hide his amusement, he roared with laughter as he turned awkwardly to face Abigail, his outstretched hand ready to receive payment. 'Wow, what a mess! I'm guessing no one's lived here for a while.'

But as her chuckling driver set about retrieving her luggage, Abigail sat numb, looking out at the neglected house, now a shadow of what her grandmother had so lovingly called home.

'Come on, then. You're still on the clock.' Her driver teased her, opening the door.

'But-but, I-I don't understand. Mr Mackay, he was supposed to be looking after the place,' Abigail insisted, more for her comprehension than her driver's.

They both stood for a moment, taking in the chaos of their surroundings. The barren landscape and its resident sheep had invaded the now overgrown driveway. The open porch that'd once elegantly mirrored the front of her grandmother's house was lost in an array of grasses, ivy, birds' nests, sheep droppings, and cobwebs. And Abigail didn't want to think about the furry little critter that'd just scuttled off into the trees behind.

What had once been a stunning home with open views across the sea loch had been swallowed up by its surroundings and, more worryingly to Abigail, wildlife had encroached, appearing to have moved into the porch at least.

'You, eh'—the taxi driver, who'd removed his cap to sort his thinning hair, was now looking more concerned than amused—'you sure you wanna stay?'

All the while, the smell of the sea air assaulted her nostrils. As the sea birds' chatter cluttered her thoughts, Abigail fought to stop her tears. 'I-I've no option.'

'Oh well, here's my card. Number's on the back if you change your mind.'

And with that, he was gone. Abigail had never felt so alone.

Chapter Two

Turning the key in the lock, Abigail couldn't quite decide if the tightening knots in her stomach were relief that her key still worked, or dread at the thought of taking that first step inside.

The opening door disturbed cobwebs, causing a spontaneous fit of coughing as dust caught in her throat. But she was relieved to see the inside of the house wasn't in quite as bad a state as the outside. There was no obvious wildlife at least, and that was an all-important positive for Abigail as she pondered her reluctance to take her luggage inside.

Choosing to leave it in the driveway for now, Abigail noticed markings made by the opening door on the dusty carpet extended further than she had opened it.

She stopped for a moment, thinking that Mr Mackay had

probably been given a key to check on things when he came to do the garden. Although, given the state of the outside, the thought niggled. It was obvious he hadn't been near the garden in years.

Tentatively, Abigail stepped across the threshold and into her past. An unexpected sense of calm enveloped her as she paused in the lifeless hall. The living room, or as her grandmother had always called it, the front room, was off to her right. It looked dated, dingy, and empty apart from the old, excessively floral sofa Abigail could remember from her childhood.

Her eyes were drawn to the panoramic window that captured the sea loch in all its glory. Images of two smaller windows, more in keeping with the island style, danced in her consciousness.

She could see herself at around six or seven years old, lying front-down on the carpet as she drew pictures for her mother. Pictures her mother would never see.

At some point during the years she can't recall, Abigail's grandmother had had the windows and a section of the wall removed, replacing it with panoramic triple-glazing that brought the sea loch into the living room.

The views were mesmerising, and Abigail knew the loch well enough to know that the view would be ever-changing as the tide came and went with the North Atlantic weather.

Crossing the hall to a much smaller room, Abigail inched into the sewing room. It was where her grandmother had spent much of her time, and Abigail didn't have to try too hard to picture her sitting at the narrow table in front of the window.

She could almost hear the heavy whirr from the sewing machine rising above her grandmother's hunched shoulders, as she rustled up another skirt or whatever garment her latest customer had ordered.

But now, the room served only to remind Abigail of her loss and the life-changing events that'd taken place within the house six long years before.

Abigail continued up the hall. Two bedrooms went off to the left and another, plus the bathroom, off to the right.

Most of her grandmother's furniture had gone. Abigail could recall that happening, although she desperately wished that memory had been swallowed up by the deep dark void along with the others.

Pulling the padded jacket tighter across her front, Abigail cringed at how the lack of clutter emphasised the patterned wallpaper and flooring, giving the house a sinister, claustrophobic feel.

Finally, the hall gave way to the open-plan kitchen with dining space. It took up the rear of the house and was bigger than she'd remembered. The electric Aga remained nestled among dated, wooden kitchen units, as did the giant rectangular dining table. Presumably because it was far too big to fit through any of the doors in one piece.

And she was relieved to see the kitchen appliances were all still in place. Not allowing herself to contemplate, even for a second, that they might not work, she flicked the switches next to the fridge and Aga and crossed her fingers.

*

The numbness she'd felt in the taxi hadn't left her. And she was overwhelmingly aware of the tasks that lay ahead if she was to ensure her grandmother's house was habitable again. The thought only added to her fragile emotions. Returning to Lochside wasn't going to be as straightforward as she'd thought. But what choice did she have? Where else could she go?

It was all becoming too much. Turning on her heels, she hurried outside to the peace and tranquillity of the sea.

And as the incoming tide's ebbs and flows danced in the moonlight, Abigail attempted to keep to the old path where possible while at the same time dodging overgrown nettles, grasses, and weeds.

Living by the sea on a Scottish island meant gardens were harder to keep. The often-cold temperatures, sea, and wind combined to create a hostile environment for many species. But, even so, there was no denying the garden had taken on a positively wild theme and Abigail was all too aware it was going to take far more than a pair of secateurs to get it straight again.

The only thing to do, she decided, as she clambered onto the rickety jetty, was to ignore it for now.

The jetty was frail, its ageing limbs evident as it slanted precariously to the left. Testing each wooden slat with her foot, Abigail proceeded further out onto the sea loch, stopping only when her grandmother's house, and its overgrown garden, had disappeared from her peripheral vision.

Shivering, she allowed the island and its painfully familiar sounds and smells to embrace her, wrapping around her as though her grandmother had just swaddled a comforting blanket around her tense, cold shoulders.

And, as the moonlight shimmered across the darkness of the hypnotic water, her thoughts were transported back in time, to her early childhood and the only years at Lochside she could recall.

Images flashed before her. Closing her eyes, Abigail could see herself as a young child. Swimming, giggling, splashing: happy!

Yes, for a short while she'd been happy here, before she'd realised her mother was never coming back for her. Then it'd become the loneliest place on the planet.

Now, as she stared into the darkness, she felt the same intolerable and overwhelming sense of confusion and abandonment she'd felt when her mother had left her as a four-year-old, standing on this very spot. No goodbye, no hug, no explanation. Tears came once more, and Abigail sobbed as though it were yesterday.

'I wouldn't stand on there if I were you. It's not looking too safe.'

Startled and disorientated, Abigail spun around. A man – early thirties, she guessed – was standing on the shore. His hands were tucked into his pockets, giving Abigail the impression that he was slightly nervous about approaching her.

He stepped closer. 'Sorry, I didn't mean to startle you. I thought you'd have heard the van. Seen the headlights?' The stranger hesitated for a moment, as if searching for something lost. But as Abigail eyed him with ambivalence, their silence seemed too much for him.

His expression changed; it was now in complete agreement with his stance. 'I'll leave. I just thought you'd...I just thought you'd be someone else, that's all. I brought supplies.'

Abigail, unsure of what to do or say, stood still, completely overwhelmed by the events of recent days.

'I still wouldn't stand there, though. I'm not sure it's safe.'

Embarrassed, and gathering herself just enough to regain a little composure, Abigail wiped her tear-stained cheeks while the stranger turned his attention to the contents of his van.

Was there something familiar in the way he moved? Was it the way he tilted his head? She wasn't sure.

'How did you know I was here?'

'My folks own the shop a couple of miles up the main road. Your taxi driver stopped. Said you were bac—eh...Said you were here.'

Silence, as each stood awkwardly waiting for the other to speak.

'Right, well. We, eh, we thought you might need some food. There's bread, milk, tea, coffee, and enough staples and cleaning supplies to keep you going for a few days until you get sorted out. There's a leaflet with the shop's number, and we deliver. Might be useful since you've no car.' He glanced around. No sign of the blue Volkswagen Golf that would normally have brought Abigail to Lochside.

Abigail watched as he placed the overflowing box on the front porch with ease. She sensed something wasn't right. 'The shop was open? At this time of night? That doesn't seem likely, not here on the island.'

'No, no, you're right. It closes at six, but the driver knocked on my parents' door. They live not far from the shop. Everyone knows everyone around here. You know how it is. I-I mean you *might* know...' He broke off.

Abigail eyed him awkwardly. Her questioning had flustered him. 'Thank you. What do I owe you?'

'I-I'm not sure.' He shrugged. 'Anyway, that's the least of your worries. You can sort that out when you phone the shop. How long are you staying?'

'Oh, for a while,' she replied, rolling her eyes.

'Well, I'd better head. But call the shop if you need anything. We used to, eh, we used to know the owner,' he added hesitantly, gesturing to the house. 'We're more than happy to help.' And then, just like everyone else, he was gone.

The owner. His words lingered as she dismounted the jetty and picked her way through the surrounding chaos to examine the contents of the newly delivered box.

Her eyes were instantly drawn to the bottle of Pinot Grigio nestled neatly between the pasta and milk, alerting her to the fact she had to get some of the contents into the fridge.

Picking up the box with far less ease than the delivery guy, Abigail carried it into the kitchen and placed it on the oversized table her grandmother had had built by a local carpenter when she was around six years old.

Tears began to flow. Only this time, for the first time since she'd woken up in a hospital bed six years ago, she allowed herself to weep uncontrollably for all she'd lost and all she'd endured, until her pounding head begged for relief.

Minutes felt like hours but, eventually, her burning eyes ran dry. She remembered where she was, and the heartbreaking curveball life had thrown at her peaceful city existence, resulting in her doing the one thing she'd sworn she would never do: return to Lochside.

Regaining her composure, she clutched her pounding forehead and turned her attention to the fridge. To her relief, the light was on and there was the slightest hint of coolness.

Once the fridge items were away, she turned on the taps. They choked and gurgled for a few seconds, but eventually water began to flow and, deciding she'd better leave them running to clear the pipes, she looked around for the light switch.

Abigail knew she should have been more involved with her grandmother's estate, but at the time, she'd wanted nothing to do with it. And, as she wandered into the bathroom to turn on the sink and bath taps and run the shower, those feelings had only intensified.

Relieved that the power was still on, Abigail searched for the hot water switch. She was becoming increasingly aware of just how lucky she was, given her first impression out in the driveway.

Glancing at her watch, she reflected on her hours of travelling as the two diamanté hands insisted it was ten forty-five.

Her gaze flitted from the claustrophobic décor to the panoramic window, and then from the loch to the woods and the dirt track that tauntingly wound its way back to civilisation, before falling on the overgrown garden and her array of mismatched luggage: still abandoned; still sitting exactly where the taxi driver had left it.

Reluctantly, Abigail began ferrying the varied pieces inside. Once it was all piled in the hall, she thought about which bedroom she should take. There was the obvious choice: the biggest of the three, which sat behind the living room. But it'd been her grandmother's. Then there was the room opposite, the one she'd used as a child, but as well as being steeped in early memories, it unnervingly reminded her of the years she'd lost.

Deciding there was only one option, she grudgingly hauled her luggage further up the hall and into the smallest of the three.

There was a bed but no bedding or pillows and, apart from a mirror stuck to the back of the door, no other furniture.

Catching sight of her reflection, Abigail barely recognised the apparition before her. Tears filled her eyes. Still dressed in the horrendous ensemble she'd arrived in, exhausted and emotionally drained, Abigail lay down on the bare mattress.

No matter how hard she tried to suppress her thoughts, the events of the previous few days, the events that'd led to her returning to Lochside, began to cruelly overwhelm her. Eventually, her tears turned to sobs, allowing an exhausted Abigail to drift into a deep sleep.

Chapter Three

Two days prior, Abigail had been sitting in her favourite restaurant, Piquant, eating lunch and sipping her way through a celebratory bottle of red, while she discussed her upcoming novel with her agent, Joanna.

Joanna Stuart-Thomas was in her late thirties and over recent years had become one of Abigail's closest friends. They'd met at a party thrown by Georgia, Abigail's first – and indisputably nutty – flatmate not long after she'd moved to London.

Georgia had been a saviour for Abigail. A bohemian chick through and through, she was always on her way to yoga or Pilates or to get another henna tattoo. But she'd quickly taken Abigail under her wing and, as well as introducing her to Joanna, had introduced her to Libby and Grace. Their eclectic group of four had quickly become a solid group of five.

Neither Abigail nor Joanna had wanted to be at the party that night. Abigail had still been getting over the traumatic events that'd led to her arriving in the city and Joanna had been getting over a breakup. But after Georgia had introduced them to each other, they'd spent the rest of the night bonding over their mutual desire for the party to be over.

They'd bumped into each other again a few weeks later and had gone for a coffee.

The two had become close friends. As Joanna got to know Abigail and a little of what she'd been through, she'd encouraged her to turn her feelings into a positive by writing them down.

What Joanna hadn't realised was that Abigail was a natural and, as well as being an emotional release, it'd taken Abigail down a path she would never have dreamed possible before. It'd been a turning point, giving Abigail a purpose and, as it turned out, a career she loved.

Five months later, when Abigail's first manuscript had landed on her desk, Joanna had been blown away by Abigail's writing style. It'd initially taken quite a bit of convincing for Abigail to agree to it being published, but five years had passed since then and Abigail hadn't looked back.

Working together had only strengthened their friendship and Joanna had been there for Abigail as she'd struggled to settle into city life. But she'd also been there, quite literally, when Abigail had walked in on Darren in bed with another woman.

Over the last twenty-four hours, the happy, bubbly world

that Abigail had fought so desperately to build after a childhood of solitude and abandonment had come crashing down with one heartbreaking drama after another. Abigail's only escape had been Lochside, the place she'd fled so dramatically six years before.

Abigail and Joanna had left Piquant high on the excitement of Abigail's sixth eagerly anticipated novel, which was due to hit the shelves in September.

Joanna had just confirmed the Lancaster Hotel for the launch, as well as a guest list that had filled Abigail with dread. Being the centre of attention was not her forte.

But when Abigail had announced she'd just finished writing her seventh novel, Joanna had been consumed with excitement and had convinced Abigail to change her plans.

So, instead of an afternoon of shopping, Abigail had found herself walking back towards her flat with Joanna to collect said manuscript. Abigail could remember giggling as Joanna had prattled on about the four delinquent stepchildren she'd acquired when she'd eventually moved in with Sam, the unlikely love of her life.

It was a side to Joanna that Abigail had struggled to relate to. Always immaculate, Joanna was an advocate of perfectly tailored trouser suits and on-brand handbags, while her perfectly straightened blond extensions never had a hair out of place.

Chasing around after children, shopping for Calpol, and doing the school run didn't compute when it came to Joanna.

But it was at this point, as they made their way to the flat Abigail shared with Darren, that her own life had begun to unravel. They'd bumped into Cleo, a sort of friend-of-a-friend of-a-friend.

Cleo's panic had quickly brought the giggling girls from their bubble as she bombarded them with the disasters that'd recently befallen her local amateur dramatics group.

Marion, the elderly vicar's wife, and star of the show, had fallen in her garden, spraining her ankle badly enough to be on crutches. Adele had stepped up as the new Marion as she was already familiar with the role. Adele's role had been quickly filled by the ever-eager Joyce, whose own role had been filled by Elizabeth. Naturally, Elizabeth's role should have been filled by Harriet but, given Elizabeth and Harriet didn't quite see eye-to-eye, no one had been surprised when Harriet had refused. Perish the thought that Harriet would be given a small and silent role!

And now what was Cleo to do? It was Friday, the final dress rehearsal night, with sold-out matinee and evening shows to follow the next day.

Abigail had watched Cleo as she recounted the cast's recent predicaments. Cleo had been in such a flap, almost airborne. Abigail had wondered how it was possible to put so much drama and hysteria into a conversation. At the same time, she reminded herself to bank the memory; Cleo would make a wonderfully eccentric character in a future novel.

Fast forward a few minutes, and she'd had her arms wrapped tightly around Abigail, gushing with far too much enthusiasm – even for Cleo – as she thanked Abigail for her apparent offer to be the stand-in for the silent role.

Abigail had no recollection of said offer. And she'd been

left reeling at the prospect, as Cleo had bid them both farewell before shouting a reminder to be at the church hall at six thirty sharp, just as she'd disappeared around a corner.

Joanna, knowing exactly how out of her comfort zone Abigail would feel on stage, tried desperately to reassure her by suggesting she pile on the make-up so no one would recognise her.

Still confounded by their unfortunate encounter with Cleo, the duo had continued their journey. Abigail had led Joanna up to the third-floor flat she'd shared with Darren for just under five years.

It'd been love at first sight for Abigail. Darren was gorgeous, funny, and kind. He could be unpredictable and a bit of a rogue at times, but Abigail liked that.

Excited to get her hands on the manuscript, Joanna had instinctively followed Abigail down the hall and into the bedroom.

Abigail had her writing corner set up: laptop, desk, printer, and a view out over the city. But Joanna hadn't known where to put herself when they'd walked in to find Darren in bed with another woman.

Understandably, Abigail had been devastated, and a war of words had ensued. Joanna had quietly retreated to the stairwell and had resisted the temptation to stick her foot out when the tearful other woman had bolted out of the door, making her bid for freedom. A few moments later, a sobbing Abigail had appeared and together they'd retreated to Joanna's.

But Abigail being Abigail, she'd refused to let Cleo down

and had turned up for rehearsals at six thirty sharp, just as instructed. It'd been an utterly horrendous evening, and she hadn't escaped again until well after eleven.

By the time she'd returned to Joanna's, she'd been unable to remember any of the instructions Cleo had given regarding her role in the play.

Fast forward again, and it's Saturday morning. Typical April showers had resulted in Abigail taking a taxi to Darren's. She'd known she didn't want him back, not after what he'd done, but she was desperate for answers.

Climbing the stairs to their flat, she'd felt an ache in the pit of her stomach and had wanted to cry for the hundredth time that morning. She'd texted him earlier to say she would be around at eleven, on her way to the matinee show. Although she could tell he'd seen her text, he hadn't responded.

But her fears had turned to devastation and yet more heartache when she'd climbed the final flight of stairs to discover her belongings piled high on the landing, in an array of carrier bags, bin bags, and cardboard boxes, and Darren nowhere to be seen.

She'd let herself in. Fuelled mostly by rage, she'd wandered around gathering the odds and ends Darren had missed.

She'd been quick to notice the extra toothbrush and toiletries in the bathroom, as well as unfamiliar clothing on the bedroom chair. Abigail had known there and then that she'd been replaced, but what had devastated her the most was the speed at which it'd been done.

Abigail had slumped onto the end of the bed. How could

she have got their relationship so wrong? In recent months, she'd been secretly hoping for a proposal. At any given moment, she'd fully expected him to drop down onto one knee as he held up a dazzling diamond solitaire ring. They'd lingered at jewellers' windows a couple of times, and she'd excitedly presumed he was getting ideas on styles.

Instead, she'd had to battle with the realisation that life as she'd known it was over. That she was homeless. And that Darren had been far too engrossed in moving New Toothbrush Girl into the flat to have been the slightest bit upset at losing her.

Abigail had known there wasn't enough time to get all her belongings across the city to Joanna's and, instead, had ferried everything around to the church hall, losing count of the number of trips it'd taken in showers that'd mocked her as each deluge had come at the most inappropriate time.

Once Abigail had made her final trip, Cleo had helped her pile her belongings in a corner, out of the way. Although Abigail had sensed Cleo's panic had been more for her show than her own predicament.

'The show must go on!' Cleo had sounded like a stuck record as she'd tried desperately to rally her unruly troops. Eventually, in a blur of noise, laughter, and applause, both shows were over. And, as the rest of the cast had revelled in their successes, Abigail had stood sobbing beside her discarded possessions.

She wasn't like other women. She didn't have childhood treasures, only what she'd accumulated since she'd moved to the city. It was mostly clothes, far too many pairs of boots, her laptop and writing paraphernalia, books, some bedding, a couple of throws, and a few pictures and trinkets she'd gathered.

She'd given up a furnished flat when she'd moved in with Darren and, until now, how much was his and how much was hers hadn't mattered.

Unexpectedly, she'd felt an arm around her. Joanna, who'd sneaked in just in time to give her moral support for the evening show, had been unaware of the day's earlier events.

'Come on, hun. Let's gather this together and get it back to mine.'

The black bags had torn in multiple places during their trip from the landing to the church hall. Every time they lifted one, its contents fell to the floor. The cardboard boxes were too wet to be reused. Abigail wept again.

The sight of her dishevelled belongings scattered around her, the feeling of isolation, of being unloved and of being homeless, all took their toll. She could not have stopped the tears if she'd tried.

Joanna had done what she could to console Abigail but what she hadn't realised was that the feeling of being completely alone in the world was not new to Abigail. She'd felt that way for much of her childhood, and over time, her writing had become both her escape and her therapy. It was the resurgence of these feelings and emotions that'd scared Abigail the most.

Joanna had grabbed a couple of old suitcases that'd been used during the show and had managed to find a couple more in a prop cupboard. All were from the 1930s and '40s, and all were well used. Joanna had been quick to discover they all had their own unique aromas too, a mixture of dust, mothballs, and old ladies, she'd decided.

As Joanna had continued to search through the various prop cupboards, she'd found a couple of plastic storage boxes, which she'd emptied and refilled with Abigail's laptop and writing paraphernalia. She'd then packed what she could of Abigail's belongings into the suitcases. But still in need of luggage, Joanna had embarked on her final search, only to return with a handful of old shopping bags. Once everything had been repacked, Joanna had called a taxi.

Abigail couldn't remember what happened after they'd left the church hall that night. She could only remember the taxi coming to a halt at traffic lights.

The darkness and the rain hammering on the windscreen had enhanced the fiery red of the traffic light, and its glare had been piercing. Dazzling as it radiated through the windscreen, it'd been at that point that Abigail knew she had to get away.

She'd known she couldn't sleep on Joanna's sofa indefinitely, especially after hearing the countless stories of her delinquent stepchildren. And, most importantly, she'd known she couldn't be anywhere where she ran the risk of running into Darren, not for a long while at least.

Frantically, she'd shouted to the driver, 'The station. The train station, please.'

Joanna had tried desperately to talk her into staying, but Abigail had been adamant. Even though she, herself, hadn't understood the pull. Instead, she'd sat silently while Joanna had run from one snack vendor to another gathering enough supplies to keep Abigail going during her trip.

'They'll have coffee on the cart. Please, please get some. Don't go to sleep and leave your stuff unattended. Promise me?' Joanna had given Abigail all sorts of instructions and, although Abigail had nodded in agreement, nothing had sunk in.

Abigail had felt numb. She had done since she'd walked in on Darren and New Toothbrush Girl. Gallingly, she was a woman Abigail had introduced him to at a book signing event almost a year before.

As the pennies began to drop, Abigail had known their affair had been going on for some time.

That's what had angered her the most. Why hadn't Darren just come clean? Why'd he not had the guts and the decency to be honest with her?

How often had this other woman been in their flat? How often had she climbed into their bed? The very thought made her feel sick.

Abigail and Joanna had sat for hours. Joanna dozing in and out of sleep, apparently afraid to leave her friend alone; Abigail switching between bouts of devastation and anger.

Initially, Abigail kept insisting that Joanna went home, but it was a battle she knew she would never win, so she'd given up.

Finally, early morning commuters had brought the station back to life. Joanne had disappeared for a short while, only to return with breakfast and a much-needed coffee before it was time for Abigail to board her train.

Joanna had frantically waved Abigail off as the busy train headed north and had texted her throughout the journey. But Abigail had just sat. Sat for miles looking out at the passing countryside as it whisked her further away from the Darren-inflicted heartache, only to be whisked ever closer to the life she'd sworn she would never return to.

Forty-eight hours was all it'd taken for Abigail's life to unravel for the second time.

There had been several changeovers during her journey. London Kings Cross to Edinburgh had gone smoothly enough, as had Edinburgh to Inverness. But it was when she'd boarded her final train from Inverness to Kyle of Lochalsh that her hackles had been raised.

Her final train was much smaller, only two carriages, and as she'd crossed the platform, she'd scanned them both in the hope of finding a quiet spot.

She'd clocked the American Tourist, engrossed in a newspaper and oblivious to the rest of the world in the busier of the two carriages. Abigail had opted for the second, less crowded carriage.

There had been numerous stops, and the curious side of the writer meant that Abigail had watched her fellow travellers as they'd embarked and disembarked at the various stations along the route.

So, when the American Tourist walked nonchalantly into her carriage as if he were a new arrival as they'd left Lochluichart at just gone seven, Abigail bristled.

Her reaction to him had taken her by surprise. She'd

become anxious. Cramps formed in the pit of her stomach. Goosebumps enveloped her body.

Sensing he was heading in her direction, she'd pulled her book from her bag. Whatever he was up to, whatever the cause of her anxiousness, Abigail was going to be seen to be engrossed. And anyway, she hadn't been in the mood for small talk.

The American Tourist had sat down beside her, tucked his rucksack behind his legs, and clasped his hands behind his head. His rugged appearance gave the impression life hadn't been overly kind to him. But still, Abigail guessed he was in his mid to late fifties.

By the time he'd settled himself into his seat, they'd reached the next station. Abigail watched an impeccably dressed gentleman board – the only person to get on at Achanalt. Keeping his head down, he'd taken a seat at the front of their carriage.

A few minutes later, the quiet carriage had been disturbed by the pinging of the American Tourist's phone. Abigail saw him type a quick response, moments before the Impeccably Dressed Gentleman rose from his seat and walked up the carriage. He took the seat opposite the American Tourist.

Abigail absorbed him in her peripheral vision. He looked as though he'd just left the set of an Italian gangster movie.

His suit and tie were pristine, his jet-black hair combed and oiled into place. She decided he was a similar age to the American Tourist, although it looked as though his life had been far kinder.

Turning another page in her book, Abigail had been aware

of their newest companion putting a black leather bag on the table that separated the two travellers. It resembled a gent's toilet bag, rectangular in shape, and zipped across the middle. It looked expensive, but Abigail wouldn't have expected anything else, given the rest of the Italian's attire.

She'd understood *Ciao* and *Arrivederci*, but the rest of the conversation had been lost on her. It'd been obvious, though, that the American Tourist was just as fluent in Italian as his acquaintance and, given how familiar they seemed to be in each other's company, Abigail decided it was fair to assume they knew each other well.

The two gentlemen had spoken for about ten minutes before their conversation became heated. The Italian businessman had finally given the American Tourist an instructive nod before disembarking at Achnashellach, leaving the black leather bag behind.

Another five minutes had then passed before the American Tourist rose from his seat, picking up his rucksack with one hand and the black leather bag with the other, all in one slick movement. He'd then disappeared into the other carriage.

What had confused Abigail, though, was that the American Tourist had returned about fifteen minutes before her stop, sat back down beside her, and placed his rucksack behind his knees. There had been no sign of the black leather bag.

Abigail knew there must be a logical explanation for such odd behaviour, but she hadn't at that time been able to put her finger on what that might be.

Chapter Four

Reaching for her duvet, Abigail's icy hand searched in vain. She was cold, stiff, and sore from sleeping without a pillow or bedding. And, she was momentarily confused as the wig, still clipped to her hair from Saturday's shows, slid around her face while she squirmed to get comfortable.

But it was the grimy trail from the remnants of her piled-on make-up, smudged across her fingers, that brought Abigail rather sharply back to reality.

Scrunching herself into the foetal position, memories of recent days came flooding back like a torrid wave. And yearning for both warmth and consolation, she got neither as the cold air led to an inner chill.

Still dressed as the silent character from the play, Abigail grabbed a blanket from one of her suitcases and wrapped it around her shivering body before hurrying to the kitchen. The Aga had warmed the room and Abigail felt her shoulders sink a little as some of the tension left her body.

Not a coffee machine in sight! Her thoughts turned to the shiny silver contraption currently sitting in Darren's kitchen. She imagined Toothbrush Girl pouring herself another espresso before climbing back into her old bed with her old boyfriend.

Abigail surveyed the kitchen. No sign of a toaster either. Convinced it couldn't get any worse, she put the kettle on to boil and placed two slices of bread onto the Aga's boiling plate.

A fleeting sense of déjà vu swept across her, as did the realisation that she'd remembered how to make toast on an Aga.

Once armed with her tea and uninspiring buttered toast, Abigail retreated to the much colder living room. Her eyes were drawn to the loch's still waters, and she found herself instinctively embracing the view.

Disorientated by the early morning daylight, Abigail glanced at the two diamanté hands, and was gutted to discover it wasn't long past six.

Scowling at the early hour, she pulled the blanket tighter around her shoulders and munched reluctantly on her toast, while at the same time, throwing an unimpressed scowl towards the open fireplace.

Apart from the fact there was no wood, she knew it couldn't be lit until the chimney had been swept. It would only take a bird's nest or two to catch aflame and the whole chimney would be up, filling the house with smoke.

It'd occasionally happened when she was a young child,

often after the first light of the winter. So, she dreaded to think how bad it would be after all this time.

Neither the stunning views, morning bird song, nor the sun's reflection on the still waters could draw Abigail from her slump as she sank further and further into the old sofa. It'd more than seen better days, and she wrestled to get comfortable, before finally allowing herself to get lost in the weekend's painful events all over again.

She was just as angry with herself as she was with Darren. How had she not seen the signs? How had she not known what Darren was up to? She was usually so aware of her surroundings, so aware of people's oddities and mannerisms, and she couldn't understand how on earth she'd missed what must have been a monumental shift in their relationship.

Drifting in and out of sleep, her thoughts and dreams became entangled and all sense of where she was had gone. She was now existing in her consciousness, revisiting the weeks and months since that fateful signing when she'd introduced Darren to *her!* When she'd unwittingly changed the course of her own life forever.

Chapter Five

Apart from the occasional visit to the kitchen, when her stomach rumbled its demands for sustenance, Abigail spent a miserable couple of days on the sofa.

At some point, she'd prised the wig from her head, but that'd been her solitary achievement and, as night fell once again and the lowering sun's shimmer remained on the still water, Abigail drifted off into another deep sleep. That is, until the sun, pouring in through the window, alerted her to yet another dreaded day.

A quick check of the two diamanté hands and, not only was it almost lunchtime, but according to the watch display, it was now Wednesday. She was also out of bread, the milk wasn't smelling too good, and she'd a craving for chocolate, cheese, and decent cereal.

Reluctantly, she opened a tin of soup and heated it, before filling a mug and retreating to the sofa. Falling back into the Abigail-shaped divot, she covered herself with the now gross blanket and sipped hesitantly at her hot soup.

In desperate need of shopping, she was grateful that the only way to get it was to call the number on the leaflet the delivery guy had left when he'd brought her groceries.

The thought of going out, of interacting with people, of having to be cheerful and polite, was unbearable. All she felt capable of, at this moment in time, was keeping herself tucked away as she metaphorically licked her Darren-inflicted wounds.

But deep-down Abigail knew she had to clean herself up. Days of living on the sofa with varying degrees of sobbing had taken its toll and, although she was deep in the depths of a broken heart, she was all too aware that still lounging around in an old theatre costume she'd first put on for Saturday's performances was the most unhygienic thing she'd ever done. The discarded mugs and plates lying scattered at her feet only served to fuel her disgust.

This wasn't her. This wasn't how she lived. She could feel her anger rise again. It was all Darren's doing. He'd inflicted this life on her, she decided moodily.

But she was also aware that, given the state of her grandmother's house, Mr Mackay had more than likely never paid a visit to Lochside.

Furthermore, and far more worryingly, that thought led her to wonder who'd caused the markings on the carpet just inside the door when she'd first arrived.

The more she thought about it, the more irritated she became. It was obvious: Mr Mackay hadn't kept to his end of the bargain and she could only hope that he hadn't been taking his agreed fee from her grandmother's estate either.

Peeling herself from the sofa, Abigail wandered to the kitchen in search of the cleaning products the delivery guy had brought with her groceries. And, given the ample supplies, it was obvious his mum was more than aware of the tasks that lay ahead.

Deciding there was nothing else for it, Abigail spent the rest of the daylight hours taking down and bagging up the old curtains, throwing rugs onto the decking in yet more clouds of dust, hoovering the entire house three times, four in some places, and dusting and wiping down the woodwork. She washed the walls, windows, and light fittings with old towels she'd found in a cupboard. She scrubbed every inch of the bathroom and kitchen before moving on to the insides of the kitchen cupboards and drawers. The contents of each were emptied and what was salvageable was washed or wiped down before being returned.

Abigail brushed, scrubbed, wiped, and rinsed. It was the only thing she could control, the only part of her life that had any direction. The pain and desolation she'd felt from the events of the last few days were now channelled into cleaning a house she hated. But the only thing Abigail knew for sure was that she did not want another morning waking up to the same mess.

As the sun lowered over the far side of the sea loch, an exhausted Abigail shut the last of the kitchen cupboards and tidied away the cleaning products and the remaining contents of the box. After deliberating the array of foods, and running low on both energy and inspiration, she opted for pasta.

By just gone ten thirty she'd had a late dinner and was pouring herself a second glass of wine. Taking it outside onto the once quaint decking, Abigail couldn't avoid the mess tauntingly illuminated in the moonlight. Ugh, the next job, she thought. Can't have the wildlife moving inside.

Deciding to follow the adage *Out of sight, out of mind,* she strolled down to the shoreline.

The dark waters rippled in the gentle breeze, while the moon's rays lit up the timeworn jetty. Abigail, surprised at her response, smiled. She could picture her grandmother sitting at the far end in her old wicker chair. It'd been her grandmother's favourite time of the day, and Abigail could almost understand why.

She resisted the temptation to clamber onto the jetty for a second time, the comments made by the delivery guy suddenly front and centre of her thoughts.

She couldn't quite decide if it was the wine or the calmness of the evening, but she was finally relaxing, finally allowing his words to sink in: *We used to know the owner!*

Thankfully, her hideous ensemble meant he'd most likely mistaken her for a frumpy eighty-year-old, and as Abigail had been in no state to chat or to have her past dragged up, that'd suited her just fine.

But she now realised she must have known him. Digging deep into the only memories she had of living at Lochside, she was acutely aware her recollections were only ever of herself and her grandmother. For Abigail, that'd always been the issue.

Shivering in the night air, Abigail wound her way back towards the house. She glanced over her shoulder to take in the shimmering water one last time, just as her grandmother would have done.

Chapter Six

When Abigail woke the following morning, she refused to allow herself to wallow any longer. Peeling herself from her bed, she went in search of her toiletries. A task that was far easier said than done given there had been no logic to Joanna's repacking in the theatre.

But having searched through the array of suitcases, storage boxes, and shopping bags, Abigail could eventually account for most of her toiletries, or enough to make do at least.

Her biggest problem was a towel. And, realising her only solution was to use a sheet from the bedding she'd brought with her, she cursed herself for not thinking to take some of the expensively soft, charcoal-grey towels currently stacked neatly in Darren's flat. After all, she'd bought them.

The thought of Toothbrush Girl wrapping herself in their

luxurious softness, having just stepped from the power shower, had Abigail muttering under her breath. Abigail was about to endure an old electric shower that had been a fixture in her grandmother's house for decades.

Deciding that, for the sake of her sanity, she couldn't continue to dwell on the antics of Toothbrush Girl, Abigail began to peel off the theatre costume.

Just removing the padded jacket alone made her feel a stone lighter. Abigail's character had been quite overweight, and her outfit had been a convincing guise.

Motionless under the warm water, Abigail felt the burden of the previous weekend begin to disappear down the plughole with the soapy suds. She realised that, although her broken heart would need time to heal, she would be okay. Life would go in whatever way fate decided. After all, she'd endured far worse.

Opting for a pair of cropped skinny jeans, a purple T-shirt to cheer herself up, and a fleece to take away the chill, Abigail began sorting through her luggage. The built-in wardrobe had no hangers but there was a shelved section down one side, and she piled her clothes neatly, saving a space for her toiletries and make-up.

Fortunately, Darren had thrown her hairdryer and straighteners onto her pile of belongings. So, as she tied her long auburn hair back into a neat ponytail, she was grateful it could look and feel its usual self, even if she didn't.

She closed the last of the empty cases and storage boxes and took them to the bedroom she'd used as a child, stacking them in a corner.

Memories raced against each other in a desperate bid to reach the forefront of her thoughts. But she ignored them all, suppressing them long enough to force them back into the deepest, darkest corners of her subconscious, for now at least.

And after a final check in the mirror, the lure of caffeine drew Abigail to the kitchen. And a few minutes later, she was sitting at the table, a mug of coffee in hand, reading through the leaflet the delivery guy had left a few days earlier.

It didn't say much about what they offered, but it made a song and dance about stocking fresh fruit and vegetables, and sourcing locally where possible. All Abigail could do was make a call.

'Good afternoon, Campbell's store. Morag speaking.'

'Hello. I'd like some groceries delivered, please.' Abigail ran through her list with the pleasant lady on the other end of the phone and wasn't in the least bit surprised to hear they didn't stock towels or a toaster.

'My goodness, that's quite a list you've got there. It'll be later this afternoon before we can deliver. What's the address?'

As soon as Abigail uttered the word *Lochside*, the woman's voice changed. 'Loch—Abigail, is that you?'

'Erm, yes, do I know you?'

'Oh. You-you probably won't remember me, but I certainly remember you. Your grandmother was one of my mother's oldest friends, you know. They were at school together.'

Abigail was silent.

'I'll tell you what, I'll just put an invoice in with the shopping and I'll see what I can do about towels for you. I'm guessing you're a little stuck down there. Do you have any company with you?'

'No, it's just me.'

Morag's words were still ringing in Abigail's ears as they said their goodbyes. She was *stuck down here!*

Abigail realised at that point that she hadn't fully thought things through, hadn't thought about the reality of living indefinitely at Lochside.

She was too far from the main road to walk for a bus, especially if she returned laden with bags. And she knew that at some point she was going to have to go into town for supplies.

But, more concerningly, she knew that if she decided to stay at Lochside, she was going to have to do something with the house.

The outside could wait, but the inside was another matter. Worn carpets and dated décor were one thing, but the lack of curtains and essential furniture was going to make things tricky.

The to-do list currently swirling around in her head was beginning to get out of control. And Abigail was all too aware that the current state of the house meant she was going to have to decide quickly whether her stay at Lochside was on a short- or much longer-term basis.

The thought of short term terrified her, as where else would she go? But longer term terrified her far more. The thought of committing to the house, to the area – to a place she'd spent the last six years fighting so hard to forget – was unimaginable, and yet she knew it was the simplest and most sensible option. For now, at least.

The house was hers! She was the reluctant owner of a spacious waterfront home set on a stunning shoreline in a beautiful part of the Scottish island, albeit somewhat neglected.

She knew she could sell it. She'd known that six years ago when she'd inherited it. But guilt had got in the way then and she sensed it would probably still get in the way now.

Originally, she'd toyed with the idea of renting it out, but that would've meant returning to redecorate and, at the time, that was out of the question.

Instead, after the eventful visit to her grandmother's solicitor for the reading of the will, Abigail had blocked out its very existence, leaving it abandoned in the woods, and her financial inheritance sitting in a bank. The thought of returning to Lochside, of delving into her past, had been incomprehensible until Saturday night when the glare from the traffic lights through the pouring rain had resulted in an overwhelming urge to run.

Chapter Seven

Zipping her fleece to her chin, Abigail combed the house for something that might work the heating. There was a small box at the back door, but no matter what buttons she pressed, nothing happened.

It may have been springtime, but wind bellowing around the rocky coastline as it hurtled in from the North Atlantic Ocean could reduce a house to an igloo in no time. And having lain empty for six years, the very bones of her grandmother's house felt damp, adding to Abigail's chill.

To escape the dampness, Abigail made another coffee and grabbed her notepad before wandering out into the late afternoon sun.

Following the garden around to the back of the house, Abigail cringed at the state of the raised vegetable beds and fruit trees. She could remember eating apples and plums straight from the trees when she was younger and had a pang of guilt at the neglected mess that lay before her now.

The fruit trees, varieties especially adapted to the island climate, had been her grandmother's pride and joy. Again, she wondered why Mr Mackay hadn't kept on top of the garden when it was obvious he'd recently been inside the house.

Deciding to ignore the panic that accompanied the rising to-do list, Abigail followed the old paths that had at one time criss-crossed neatly between the raised beds, eventually ending up at the old wooden garage and shed.

Both were locked. Aware of her bare ankles, she attempted to dodge the nettles as she crept down the side of the garage. All the while hoping to see if there was anything of use through the windows.

She'd hoped to find her grandmother's car. Instead, all she could make out were garden tools and her old pink bike from when she was a young child. The pink and purple ribbons her grandmother had attached to the handlebars still hung limp and enveloped in cobwebs.

Deciding she'd had enough of the overgrown garden, Abigail sipped at her coffee and ventured into the sparse, but encroaching, woodland.

She stepped precariously over the uneven ground and found herself surrounded by an assortment of birch, beech, and oak trees. Each one was unique, and beautifully distorted in shape, thanks to the island winds that'd stunted their growth.

Closing her eyes, she felt a comforting tingle spread through her body. It was as though her grandmother was standing beside her, breathing the same sea air, listening to the same swooshing of the leaves as they danced in the island breeze. For the first time in six years, Abigail felt her grandmother's presence, as though they were sharing the same blissful moment.

But a single tear trickling down her cheek reminded her of the cruel realities of life and why she'd fled, why she'd returned, and why she was alone.

Yet the hand she'd been dealt and the life she'd been forced to lead had given Abigail a self-preserving power. Although, sometimes, she found that pushing fear and heartache deep into her subconscious was a skill that was more easily said than done.

But in this instance, Abigail was able to return her attention to the beauty of the trees with little effort. Their intoxicating aromas filled her nostrils as she wandered further into the sparse wood. She stepped carefully on the uneven, cushioned grass as she went.

Startled sheep threw her an annoyed bleat before scampering out onto the dirt track that led back to the house, reminding her to watch where she put her feet.

As a small child, Abigail had found the wandering sheep only added to the island's charm. They were a part of day-to-day life. She would often give them names and talk to them as she played by the shore or wandered through the trees.

But today, as they wandered aimlessly across the dirt track without giving Abigail a second glance, she was lost in her own past.

Memories of playing hide-and-seek among the trees with her grandmother, collecting kindling for the fire, looking for wild garlic, sorrel, and occasionally, mushrooms – once her grandmother had assured her they were safe to eat – surged to the fore. And in an instant, they were quashed.

Having successfully navigated back through the encroaching trees and sheep droppings, Abigail continued down to the water. And as she clambered onto the old jetty, she made sure she was still over solid ground before she sat down.

With her legs dangling just above the supporting boulders, she shuffled through the scribbled pages of her notepad in search of an empty page. It was time to create a pros and cons list.

The pros came easily at first. Miles away from Darren, no rent or mortgage to pay, a fresh start, and, apart from travelling for book events, everything to do with her writing could be done online.

Struggling to think of another pro, Abigail turned her attention to the cons list. Joanna was at the top, followed by Libby, Grace, and Georgia. Just scribbling their names reminded Abigail that not only had she forgotten to text Joanna to let her know she'd arrived safely on Sunday night, but she'd also forgotten to tell the others she'd left.

Jumping to her feet, she ran back to the house in search of her phone, only to find it was out of battery. Plugging it in to charge, Abigail reached for her laptop before instantly putting it down again when she realised there was no Wi-Fi. A massive con right there, she thought, as she made her way back to the jetty. Although, she knew that having no Wi-Fi was a con that could be rectified quickly.

Adding it to the cons list, along with complete redecoration, carpets, curtains, furniture, new bed and bedding, towels, kitchen supplies and, underlined twice, a new sofa, meant that Abigail was beginning to feel overwhelmed.

Reality was kicking in as she added a third column. Whether she decided to stay, rent the house out, or sell it, there was no getting away from the fact that the house was badly in need of a new kitchen and bathroom.

Her thoughts turned quickly to the location of the house: midway between the head of the loch and the open water. She added remoteness to the cons list, underlining it twice. It made her feel small and insignificant as she sat perched on a jetty dwarfed by an icy ocean.

Looking out at the cold, bleak, beautiful distance, Abigail was pleased that the weather was clear enough for her to see the Outer Hebrides. Stunning yet formidable, they were the last line of defence against the harsh North Atlantic Ocean. Knowing there was no other land until the icy waters hit Canada only added to Abigail's feeling of isolation.

A scattering of cottages that could be counted on one hand dappled the rocky shoreline, before giving way to turbulent open waves.

Again, Abigail was reminded of how different her life would be if she committed to the island. Life in London had been bustling. Had felt centric and involved. A stark contrast to the stunning, restful, inspiring beauty of the Isle of Skye.

With writerly attention, Abigail noticed seagulls squawking high above the waves, ducks bobbing nonchalantly beneath the jetty, and sheep bleating as they roamed the island without a care to human restrictions or boundaries, all coming together in pathetic fallacy as if to emphasise that, yes, she was alone. That this was her throw of the dice. She had to decide whether she was going to settle for the hand fate had dealt, or whether she was going to fight against it and create a new existence, a million miles from the island, London, and everything she knew.

But as she remembered the guy who'd surprised her with shopping the night she'd arrived, she was taken aback as her thoughts turned to how her life would pan out if she decided to stay on the island.

Recalling his words that he was from the village shop *a couple of miles* up the road, Abigail dug deep into her childhood. What village shop? What village? Were there other shops? Had it always been there? She thought it odd she couldn't remember it, given she was sure she could remember her early childhood in all its turbulent glory.

But Abigail knew the answers to her questions were irrelevant. As was the decision on whether she should stay at Lochside or sell.

At some point in the not-too-distant future, Abigail would have no option but to visit the mysterious village that lay just a couple of miles from Lochside. Which led to her next – and biggest – con: no transport. Her cons list had become problematic.

Abigail's continual fight against her upbringing meant she'd become inordinately independent. If she needed something, she bought it. If something needed to be done, she did it. But the lack of transport was going to make that exceedingly difficult at Lochside. Although, she was mildly optimistic that once her phone had charged, she would discover she had a data connection and could access the internet.

Discarding her notepad and pen on the jetty, Abigail absorbed her surroundings. The tide was out. Black rocks, smoothed over time and dappled with lichen, had become exposed, providing a lolloping spot for seals as they rested, played, and slept.

Oystercatchers strutted purposefully along the shore, making the most of the exposed rocks and water pools before the tide returned to submerge them once again.

As a child, Abigail had loved the rhythm of the sea. The ebbing and flowing of the waves as the tide came and went. The dependable cycle: living, breathing, as though it had its own beating heart. Reassuringly constant. One of the few constants in her shallow pool of memories.

Abigail shifted her gaze towards the open water's abyss. The tumultuous April sky reflecting against glistening water invoked memories. Memories from her childhood attempted to resurface and, once again, she fought to suppress them.

Only this time, her efforts were futile. Hugging at her knees as if to self-comfort, she could hear her laughter, could hear the splash as she ran up the jetty and jumped into the water. She could see her tiny yellow swimming costume and the pink armbands her grandmother had insisted she wore. She could hear her grandmother chuckle as she watched from the porch and could smell the warm cocoa her grandmother handed her as she returned, shivering from the icy waters.

Images from Abigail's past flashed before her. Visions of her baking her favourite cakes with her grandmother, playing card games with her grandmother, and exploring the woods with her grandmother. Always with her grandmother, never her mother.

She saw the Christmases where her mother had let her down yet again, the cuddles her grandmother had given to comfort her, and she heard the furious telephone conversations her grandmother had had when she'd begged her daughter to come and be a mother to Abigail.

Then, suddenly, she could see her grandmother clutching at her chest. Abigail's only constant in her insular little world had gone.

'Hi. Hello.'

Abigail spun around. The delivery guy from Sunday was standing just a few feet away. With tears cascading freely, she jumped to her feet.

'Sorry, I didn't mean to startle you.'

'It's okay. I just didn't hear you arrive, that's all.'

Aware he was watching, she tried unsuccessfully to regain her composure. 'I, eh…I was just watching the water, sorry.'

'You okay?' The delivery guy looked uneasy.

Abigail couldn't help but feel sorry for him. After all, what on earth was he supposed to do with a snivelling female? 'Yeah, I…' Abigail fumbled around for words but was unable to finish her sentence.

The delivery guy came to her rescue by returning to his van and opening the rear doors. 'I have shopping for you. Quite a bit, actually.'

Abigail followed. 'A toaster. You have a toaster!' She spotted the box with the shiny appliance plastered across its front. 'But how? The lady said she didn't stock them.'

'Eh, yeah, that was my mum. We got it from the hardware shop in Portree. There are towels here too. We've paid for them and added them to your invoice. Mum said to say she hoped white was okay. She figured they'd go with anything.'

'That's so kind of her! Will you thank her for me?'

The delivery guy didn't comment. Instead, he grabbed the closest box of groceries and headed towards the porch. Abigail grabbed the toaster and followed. Opening the door, she led him to the kitchen.

As he put his box on the table, Abigail was aware of him giving the place a good once-over before walking towards the window.

'I can remember us picking apples from the trees and eating them before lunch, when your grandmother wasn't looking.'

Abigail's stomach lurched.

'You don't remember me, do you?'

Silence. Confusion. Cramps churning in the pit of her stomach.

'It's okay. It was a long time ago. I mean, I'm offended,' he joked, 'but I'll get over it. Come on, let's get the rest of the boxes.'

Abigail followed. Still silent. Racking the depths of her

limited past. Searching for a memory that included anyone other than her grandmother.

A couple more trips saw the last of the shopping into the kitchen and Abigail found herself offering her non-stranger a coffee as a thank you for going to the effort of getting her a toaster and towels.

Her words had escaped her lips before she'd had the chance to tell herself it wasn't a good idea, and there was no going back once he'd accepted.

By the time she'd made their coffee, he'd taken a seat at the table. Joining him, she mustered enough courage to ask the polite question, even if it did risk opening the floodgates to more memories.

'I'm sorry, how should I know you?'

Glancing towards her, he hesitated.

Unable to decipher his expression or comprehend his unease, Abigail realised that possibly it'd been a question too far. A question too painful to answer. After all, she knew enough to know that something traumatic had led to her having dissociative amnesia. 'I'm sorry, should I not have asked?'

Here she was, sitting beside a man who may be able to fill in her missing years, and here he was, holding on to something she could only presume was so horrendous he dared not answer.

'No, no, it's okay. From the ages of four to about eleven, we were inseparable.'

Inseparable! The thought that someone who insisted he was so integral to her childhood should be absent from what she was sure were her only true memories shook her to her core.

64

Studying his face, his eyes, his mouth as he spoke, but not seeing the slightest flicker of recognition, was frustrating. How could she not remember him? The ages of four to eleven were the only years from her first twenty-three that she could remember. And yet, if what he said was true, then even these memories were flawed.

All too aware there were only two reasonable explanations, Abigail fought quickly to decide if the stranger now sitting at her kitchen table was lying to her. That in some way he knew of her situation; it was a small island after all. Or, unthinkably, were Abigail's only memories – the ones she feared to recall while at the same time being loath to forget – were they incomplete?

Seeming to sense her conflicting emotions, the stranger reached into his pocket and pulled out his wallet.

Abigail tensed at his obvious reluctance.

'I don't want to scare you, but'—he gave Abigail a small, tattered photograph—'do you recognise either of us?'

Staring into the faded photograph, Abigail saw her eleven-year-old self, sitting on the porch, as she'd so often done as a child. Beaming a smile so bright. Abigail had forgotten she'd ever been so happy.

Sitting beside her, a boy. Similar in age, maybe a year or so older. Sporting a smile just as joyful as her own.

They were young, but as Abigail studied the picture, she could tell the child in the photograph was now the stranger sitting in her kitchen. Drinking her coffee, she said, 'I'm sorry, I don't remember you.'

'Well, I'd like to think I was pretty hard to forget, but

if you've blotted me out too, then so be it,' he joked, before abruptly lifting his head. 'Oh, I'm sorry, Abigail. I didn't mean it that way.'

Abigail realised instantly that he knew far more about her than she'd like and, if she were honest, he also knew more about her existence at Lochside and the reasons she fled than she did.

'Really, I am sorry,' he reiterated, flushing red, the regret on his face evident to see.

'It's okay. I-I don't remember much, so don't take it personally.'

Changing his tone, and giving her a smile that was oddly comforting, he stretched out his hand. 'Hi, I'm Jamie. Pleased to meet you.'

Shaking his hand, she couldn't help but laugh, relieved he'd changed the subject and lightened the mood for the second time.

The pair spent the next half hour chatting over their coffee. Abigail was relieved that he seemed just as reluctant as she was to delve into her past. But she had to admit, he was good company, easy to chat to, and she wondered if that was down to their past.

Again, Abigail found herself scrutinising his mannerisms and facial expressions as he spoke. Desperately hoping for a flicker of recognition. Still nothing.

'Please tell me you intend to do something with the décor in here,' he joked.

'What, you mean you don't like it? Well, as hideous as this is, the kitchen is the least of my worries.'

'You mean there's worse?'

'I take it you've been in here before.'

'Yeah, loads, before…Eh, yeah, years ago.'

'Well, go have a look for yourself and tell me where on earth you think I should start.'

Taking his coffee with him, Jamie sauntered into the hall. 'Does that mean you're sticking around then?' he called back.

'I don't have much choice.' Tightening her grip on her mug, she squirmed, hoping he didn't delve any deeper.

But once again, his laughter brought her from her thoughts. Following what was now an amused chuckle, she found Jamie in the living room. 'Well, what's your diagnosis?'

'A bulldozer!' He grinned. 'Although, a museum might be interested in the sofa.'

'Very funny!' But as she looked around, her mood took a slump. 'I'm dreading the work that lies ahead, and the time it'll take to make the house habitable again.' Tightening her ponytail, as though it was the one thing she could control, she was surprised at how easily she was opening up to Jamie. 'I've started a list, but I've no idea where to begin. The whole thing feels a bit overwhelming, if I'm honest.'

'Well, if you like, I could take a look. Help you work out who around here could help. There's a couple of good plumbers on the island, and an electrician up in Dunvegan. They're reliable and would do a good job.'

'That'd be great, but the priority is the heating. I can't decide if it's broken or just switched off.'

Jamie handed her his mug and went in search of the boiler, eventually finding it in a cupboard by the back door. She watched him fidget with switches and heard him swear a little while squeezing himself in between the boiler and the confusion of dials and buttons on a board on the wall. At one point, he ran out to his van, only to return a few minutes later with a couple of tools.

Abigail left him to it and set about putting the shopping away. She could feel herself relaxing a little, knowing she had food in the house.

'Heating's on,' Jamie announced, returning to the kitchen to wash his hands. 'It's on for the rest of the day, but I've set the timer to come on for a few hours in the mornings and again in the evenings. I'll show you how it works in case you want to change the times later on.'

Abigail could hear the reassuring hum as she neared the boiler. 'Oh, thank you. What did you do?'

'Not much, it was just needing a bit of a wake-up, that's all. It should take the chill off the house in no time.'

'Well, thank you. I can't tell you how relieved I am. It's been freezing, especially in the mornings. Is that what you do? Boilers?'

Jamie laughed. 'No, but I was a mechanic in the army, so a machine's a machine I guess.'

'Ah, so that's why I don't remember you?'

A fleeting expression fell across his face, but again she couldn't decipher it.

'I joined when I was twenty-five and came out at the end of last year. I plan to buy, do up, and sell old boats, and get them back out on the water. Thought I'd try and get a bit of life back into the old loch here, but I've ended up helping mum out at the shop while my dad recovers from a knee operation. A few more weeks, though, and he should be back at work, and I'll be free to get started on the boats.'

A mechanic in the army. Suddenly, the ease with which he moved the heavy boxes around made sense.

'I know someone who can bring you a load of logs and sweep your chimney while he's here. I can ask him if you like?'

'Yeah, that would be great.'

'And I'm not too sure about some of the wiring in here either. You might want to put electrician near the top of your list.'

'Yeah, I thought as much.' She sighed. 'My grandmother never seemed to make my life easy when she was alive, so why should she start now? I'm sure she's up there looking down on me, watching to see if I can rise to the challenge.'

'Yeah, that sounds like her, all right. By the way, do you want to tell me the story behind the old lady disguise on Sunday?'

She spluttered, choking on the last of her coffee. 'A story for another time' was all she could manage as she blushed a vibrant shade of scarlet and wiped the dripping coffee from her chin.

Chapter Eight

As Jamie drove the few miles between Lochside and his home at the head of the loch, his conversation with Abigail gnawed at his conscience.

It'd been reminiscent of the conversations he'd had with her when she'd woken up in the hospital six years ago, when he'd found himself caught between the explicit instructions of the doctors and medical professionals who'd cared for Abigail and his own broken heart.

His love for her had never faltered, but for the second time since she'd returned, she'd looked at him as though he were a stranger.

For six years, he'd hoped upon hope that her memories would return. That she would come rushing back to him. But, not once, in all that time, had he considered that she might still be suffering with amnesia.

As the days had turned into weeks, the weeks into months, and the months into years, he'd resigned himself to the fact that her memories had returned. And she'd either changed her mind about him or the thought of returning to Lochside had been far too painful.

And he would've understood that too. But, knowing Abigail as he did, he thought she would've at least contacted him. Given them the chance to discuss their future or explore the option of him moving to be with her.

But now, he'd no idea what to think or how to react. Seeing her so upset, still grieving over her lost years, was heart-rending.

His instincts had been to sweep her into his arms. Tell her everything would be okay and that they would get through it together. But, to her, he was merely a stranger. A stranger in a familiar landscape. He would have to keep reminding himself of that.

He wasn't long home when there was a knock at the door.

'Jamie, are you here, love?'

'In the kitchen, Mum.'

He filled the kettle, knowing that after a long day in the shop, his mum would need a cup of tea. She'd been running the shop without his dad's help for weeks and, although she never complained, Jamie could see she was feeling the strain.

'You okay, son?' Morag asked, falling eagerly into a chair at the kitchen table.

'Yeah.'

'She still didn't recognise you?'

He shook his head as he added the milk and handed her a mug of perfectly brewed tea.

'Any idea why she's back?'

'No, she's upset about something. I just can't work out what. She knew her grandmother had died when she left, so it's not that. It's something more recent, I'm sure of it.'

Putting her hand on his arm, she said, 'I'm sorry, son. I don't know what else you can do other than be there for her as a friend.'

'But I'm not a friend,' he insisted. 'I'm a stranger.'

'You will be, son. I know you. You'll want to make sure she's okay. Just give it time, and you never know, just being with you again might jolt some memories.'

Nodding, he let out a sigh as he tinkered with his mug. 'I know, I just need to watch what I say and remember what the doctors told us about not forcing her memories. I've already put my foot in it a couple of times.'

'Please, be careful, son. You have to consider yourself in all this too, you know.' Gulping the last of her tea, she placed her mug in the sink. 'I'd better get back. Your dad will be needing his next lot of painkillers and he'll need to eat first. If I'm not back, he'll have a go at cooking something himself. He's not good at following the doctor's orders. Doing nothing doesn't compute with your dad.'

Jamie laughed. 'No, I know. I'll nip in to see him in the morning before starting at the shop. If I'm not there before the delivery arrives, leave the heavy boxes for me.'

'Thanks, son. It's appreciated.'

As he saw his mum to the door, she turned to hug him. 'It'll all work out in the end. These things always do. It's, well, it's just the getting there that can be the tough bit.'

Waving her off, Jamie looked out across the water. Being nestled at the head of the loch, his home had an all-encompassing view of the loch and its spectacular surroundings. His boatyard was just a mile along the coast. Open water and the Outer Hebrides straight ahead and, if he dared look down to the distant left, Lochside. Retreating into the house, he rubbed his face in his hands, as if it would bring clarity, before sinking into a chair.

The living room was spacious enough for a small island cottage, not decorated as he would've liked, but then it was hard decorating a home you had picked out with someone else.

A text message interrupted his thoughts. He took his phone from his pocket. Claire, again. He'd only met her a couple of weeks ago while delivering shopping, but her texts were getting more familiar with each passing day, and he knew she was encouraging him to ask her out.

The attraction had been purely one-sided. He'd found her cold, distant, and frankly quite sharp, like she always expected to get what she wanted, when she wanted it. Not his type at all. In fact, he'd been gobsmacked when her first message had pinged through. Now, the pinging had become relentless.

Placing his phone screen down, he turned his attention towards the mantelpiece. The solid, natural wood sitting just above the open fireplace had caught his eye when he'd first viewed the cottage.

But it still sat bare. No ornaments; they hadn't got that far. Just a silver frame. Abigail was looking at him, the way she always had. Full of hope, full of excitement, full of love. The diamond solitaire sparkling on her left hand reminded him of their love and commitment to each other, just as they were about to embark on a life together.

Chapter Nine

Abigail's crossed leg swung nervously as she waited for Mr Houston to return. His office wasn't overly inviting. It was sparsely decorated, had what could only be described as a beige theme, and was almost in as much need of a lick of paint as Lochside.

Pictures of staff who'd come and gone over the years adorned its walls in a selection of mismatched frames, along with an array of certificates and posters. The posters all boasted the same slogan: *Making your money work for you!* Abigail couldn't help but wonder if they'd been doing that for her. Goodness knows, she needed them to come up trumps today.

Abigail had spent the last several weeks gathering quotes from contractors and decorators and had surprised herself at how much she'd enjoyed scanning brochures and websites for kitchen and bathroom ideas. But, more importantly, she'd already decided on the *pièce de résistance*: a brand-new sofa. Elegant, comfortable, inviting: in other words, everything her grandmother's was not!

'Sorry to keep you, Miss Sinclair.' Mr Houston's mop of greying curls swayed into place as he took his seat. 'Thank you for coming back in. I've got everything here.' He gestured, nodding towards the paperwork he was splaying out across his desk. 'I'll get bank cards sent out to you, but you might also want to consider moving your savings to a higher interest account. Oh, I'm just going to get you a printout of your balances and then we can take things from there. I'll just be a few minutes.'

Abigail felt her silence deafening as Mr Houston gave her a polite nod before leaving the room again. She couldn't remember much about the discussions around her grandmother's will, but she could certainly remember her mother's appearance and her ensuing tantrum.

She could remember wanting nothing to do with the mother who'd always been far too busy for her, had shown no interest in either her or her grandmother, but who'd somehow miraculously found the time to attend the reading of the will.

Abigail could remember her mother's outrage at finding out she'd been disinherited. But more so, she could remember overwhelming feelings of abandonment and the constant feeling of hindrance and inconvenience, all at the hands of her mother. An immense sense of isolation had overtaken Abigail as she battled to come to terms with the loss of a grandmother who'd kept her hidden away. She needed to escape, to be free.

The final straw had been when her mother had knocked on her grandmother's door, just a few short hours after the reading of the will.

Behind her had been a beaten-up van with a guy twenty years her junior at the wheel. The knocks and dents scattered around the van had revealed numerous layers of paint, alluding to its many lives.

Her mother had charged around the house, pointing to all the pieces of furniture she was taking. In less than an hour, her mother and her younger companion had picked the house clean. That left Abigail with nothing more than a bed, the much-too-large-for-the-van kitchen table, the hideous sofa, and some bits and bobs her mother seemed to consider unworthy of her attention.

Abigail's response had been to be vague and uncooperative, to almost disinherit herself in response to her mother's nonsense, and to move as far away as she'd dared from the home that'd felt like a prison.

'Here we are, Miss Sinclair. The balances to your three accounts. Now, these are the two smaller accounts'—he pushed two slivers of paper across his desk towards Abigail—'and this is the savings account.' Abigail glanced at the final piece of paper as Mr Houston slid it towards her. She struggled to read the other two until he sat back, withdrawing his chubby fingers.

Her face flushed as she added the balances together. 'Why are there three? Was the money not just transferred from my grandmother's account into a new one in my name?'

'Yes and no. You already had this account.' He pointed to

an account that held just over twenty thousand pounds. 'It was set up by your grandmother not long after you were born. She paid into it every month, varying amounts until she died.

'This next account holds what was in your grandmother's current account at the time her estate was settled, plus the accrued interest, and the same with her savings account.' He pushed the printouts closer towards her. 'These were transferred into comparable accounts in your name at the time. Your grandmother was fine financially. She'd no money worries to speak of, and she managed to save a decent amount each month.'

Abigail wasn't surprised. She couldn't remember her grandmother going anywhere other than into town to buy the weekly shopping.

'I remember her coming in here, you know, as far back as when I was a young lad out on the front counter. She used to take the mick out of my Edinburgh accent. Said I sounded posh. I've lost that now.' He chuckled. 'Been here too long. But she'd a heart of gold. Took no messing, mind. She'd soon put you in your place.'

Abigail laughed. 'Yeah, that was for sure.'

'Well, anyway.' Mr Houston rose and ushered Abigail towards the door. 'You'll receive your new debit cards in the post. If you haven't received anything in around three weeks, come back in, but it should all be straightforward from here.'

Abigail shook his outstretched hand. 'Thank you again for your time, Mr Houston.'

'My pleasure, Miss Sinclair.'

But just as Mr Houston was about to close the door, Abigail

interjected. 'You said you can remember my grandmother coming into the bank?'

'Yes, yes I can.'

'Was I ever with her?'

Mr Houston stood for a moment. 'No, not that I can recall. She was always alone.'

Abigail thanked him again and left. Glancing at the two diamanté hands, she was relieved to see she still had about forty-five minutes before she was due to meet Jamie.

Jamie was now in the habit of offering Abigail a lift when he was coming into Portree; it'd been a lifeline for her. And she was now at the point where locals recognised her and said their hellos, something that both pleased and haunted Abigail.

Were they merely saying hello because she'd become a familiar face, a regular customer, a resident? Or did they recognise her from her past years on the island? Had she known them previously to say hello to? Or would she have stopped and chatted? Was she now therefore seen as peculiar and rude?

It was a thought that, like so many others, Abigail pushed to the darkest recesses of her mind. She left the bank and headed towards the waterfront and the café that'd become a regular pit stop during her trips into town.

Doing her best to avoid tourists as they spilled onto the street from yet another tour bus, Abigail skirted between the hanging baskets that draped the café windows and doors and the old whisky kegs with trailing ivy elegantly falling towards the pavement. It was a reluctant reminder of the shambles she'd left at Lochside, and she felt her face crumple at the thought of the work that still lay ahead of her, both inside and out.

Only one table was available when Abigail walked into Miranda's, and she was quick to hang her gilet over the back of a chair before turning to inspect the cake counter and the specials board. After ordering a latte and a fudge doughnut, she took her seat and looked out at the busy street.

It was now mid-June and the tourist season, which never really stops on the island, was moving into full swing. The writer in her couldn't help but watch as visitors of all nationalities flocked towards the waterfront.

Some would capture the mesmerising scenery as they looked out across Loch Portree and the Sound of Raasay. Others would join queues for the much-anticipated boat trips that would take them in search of whales, dolphins, puffins, eagles, and more.

But as Abigail continued to survey her surroundings, she was taken aback at her feeling of belonging. Was she beginning to see herself as a local, an islander? Was she beginning to see the island as home?

Her thoughts turned to Mr Houston and her visit to the bank. Relief was setting in. Her grandmother had left her enough money to cover the cost of a new kitchen and bathroom, the redecoration, new flooring, and possibly some of the furniture, if she was careful.

She had her savings, the account her grandmother had left in her name and, although she hadn't written a word since the day she'd walked in on Darren and Toothbrush Girl, she still had royalties coming in from her book sales.

'Here you go, love. Enjoy.'

'Thank you.' She returned Miranda's smile.

Watching the world go by, Abigail sipped her coffee and indulged in what she quickly decided was an excellent choice of cake. She thought about the time that'd passed since she returned to Lochside and couldn't quite believe it'd only been eight short weeks since she'd struggled off the train at Kyle of Lochalsh.

And as if to add to the moment, the red glow of the traffic light at a pedestrian crossing caught her eye. How innocent it looked compared to the night she'd left London.

The traffic began to flow again, but only to stop suddenly as an elderly local decided it was her turn to cross the road.

She watched the driver's reaction as he signalled to the elderly lady to get out the way. Abigail laughed as the elderly lady shook her stick indignantly at him while still looking straight ahead, continuing at her own slow, sauntering pace. The impatient driver shook his head in return.

But Abigail looked closer, lowering her mug to the table as she leaned forward, as though it would somehow enhance her vision.

Concluding her sloth-like meander across the road, the elderly lady struggled onto the pavement and the impatient driver zipped around her and continued his journey. His car advanced closer. Abigail was in no doubt: the driver was her American Tourist!

'Thought I'd find you here!'

Startled, Abigail spun around to see Jamie ordering himself

a flat white and a slice of millionaire shortbread. By the time she looked back outside, the American Tourist's car had gone. Damn it, she thought to herself, trying desperately to decide what make of car he'd been driving and kicking herself for not taking a mental note of the number plate.

She had no idea why, but her intuition had told her he was no good the minute he'd walked into her carriage. And she was convinced he was the source of an intriguing story.

'You're a bad influence, you are. I'd never have stopped for coffee or cake until you started hogging a lift. I'll need to go for a run later. Work this off.'

'Ooh, will you have time before your hot date?'

'Oh yeah, that. I'll just have to make time.' He frowned. 'How did you get on at the bank?'

'Actually, alright. The accounts are all in my name, so all they've to do now is send out the bank cards.'

'That's great. You're all set to get started properly at the house, then?'

Nodding, she took a sip of coffee to help push down the last of her fudge doughnut. 'Yeah, I just need to chase up a few more quotes. Everyone's lovely, but everything's much more relaxed up here. It all seems to take so much longer than back in London, or maybe it's just my impatience?'

'That can be a good thing, you know.'

'What?'

'The slower pace.'

'I know,' she replied drolly, rolling her eyes. 'And, surprisingly, I seem to be succumbing to this island life again.

I just need my bank cards to come through and get set up on the banking app so that I can start moving forward. Oh, and'—she sipped at her coffee—'there's a bit more money there than I'd expected too.'

'Enough to give you the option to stay?'

'Yeah. There's enough to put in a new kitchen and bathroom, replace the dodgy windows, and put in a new back door. You know, one that'll open properly.' She chuckled.

Picking at the crumbs left by another of Miranda's delicacies, Jamie laughed. 'Yeah, that'd be a good idea!'

'It'll also cover the redecoration without touching my own money, maybe even enough to buy some new furniture if I'm careful.'

'But that's great, isn't it? Surely that gives you the choice of redecorating to sell or redecorating and furnishing to stay.'

Abigail stared into her coffee. The decision to stay was going to have to be based on far more than whether she could afford to furnish and live at Lochside afterwards. 'Jamie, do you ever remember my grandmother bringing me into Portree with her? The bank manager could remember her clearly, but I was never with her.'

The frustration at having no answers, no memories, no feeling or recognition of an existence that moulded her into who she was today: all of this overwhelmed Abigail, and this was one of those moments.

She'd found it much easier to ignore these feelings in London. But now she was back on the island, the sounds and smells that insisted on enveloping her wherever she went felt agonisingly familiar in what was mostly an alien landscape.

Turning to Jamie, Abigail wondered whether the pain and anguish she felt was visible. 'Why have I no memories of being anywhere other than Lochside? Why did my grandmother never take me with her? Surely, I was too young to be left at home alone when I first came to stay. And-and what about school, have I forgotten that too or did I never go?'

She cupped her face in her hands. 'Why would I remember my childhood but not remember school? And-and why can't I remember my teenage years? They've gone. All of them.' She choked, her exasperation getting the better of her. 'There's nothing but a black, desolate void. Right up until my early twenties. The only memories I have are when I was very young, then nothing until the day my grandmother had her heart attack.'

Jamie caressed her shoulder. He knew her pain. He knew her heartache, and he certainly knew the contents of Abigail's lost years. But the doctor's instructions still rang loudly in his head as though it was yesterday. He knew he couldn't prompt; he could only encourage.

'Do you remember anything from the day your grandmother had her heart attack? Or anything leading up to it?'

'No! I just remember her collapsing at the entrance to the hospital. Why, is there something I should know?'

'Abigail, I-I…'

'What?' she urged.

'I-I…How would I know? I'm only a year older than you,'

he joked. 'Anyway, come on.' He tilted his mug to get the last of the foam from his coffee. 'I've got a hot date tonight, remember.'

'Ooh, what you gonna wear?' She teased him again, rising from her chair to pay. Jamie followed, but she insisted it was on her this time. It was the least she could do after yet another free ride into town.

Chapter Ten

Abigail leaned back into her grandmother's old wicker chair, forcing herself, once again, to mull over her plans for her future. The glass of red in one hand and the notebook in the other did nothing to encourage her to keep on topic.

She'd spent the evening clearing a small patch of the porch to allow her to set out her grandmother's favourite chair and a small garden table.

The lure of the summer evenings and the sea air had been calling and now, so long as she ignored the surrounding shambles, she was able to enjoy the stunning views across the water and the mountains beyond.

Closing her eyes, she listened. The sound of the water ebbing and flowing in the breeze only added to the tranquillity. Taking a deep breath, she absorbed the moment. Inhaling the sea air. London felt a million miles away.

She drifted back to the all-important decision: was she going to stay or was she going to go? The words danced around in her head, and before long she'd gone completely off topic and was singing 'Should I Stay or Should I Go' by The Clash.

Was it the red wine or the tranquil June evening that was making her feel as though she was settling into life at Lochside rather too smoothly? She couldn't decide, but she knew she was continually struggling to focus on what was supposed to be the serious topic at hand.

She'd been relishing every minute of planning and renovating the house, and it was all coming surprisingly easy to her. She could imagine how each room would look once all the work was completed. Yet she was wary. She was starting to think about trinkets and artwork, purchases she wouldn't be making if she decided to sell.

Jamie had put her in touch with a couple of electricians; she'd received their quotes. Martin, who lived on the outskirts of Portree, was poised to start the rewiring on Monday.

She had a plumber starting the bathroom on Tuesday and the kitchen was being delivered and fitted in a couple of weeks. Her most trying challenge recently had been stripping the layers of wallpaper from every wall in the house. She'd never been one for perfectly manicured and painted nails, but even she was disgusted at the state her hands were in.

Abigail desperately tried to clear The Clash from her head, focussing instead on the pros and cons list she'd started when she'd first arrived at Lochside.

A few of the cons had been scored out. She was now connected to Wi-Fi; that alone had erased a few of the smaller cons from the list. But they'd quickly been replaced by others.

Cool air shivered across her skin, alerting her to the fact it was getting late. Abigail checked the diamanté hands: 9.25 p.m. Hurrying inside, she grabbed a cosy fleece and topped up her glass. Despite the coolness, sitting out on the decking was still far more inviting than huddling in the empty house.

As she passed her grandmother's old sewing room, something made her stop. Small and oddly shaped, the little room came into her mind every time she thought about writing. The atmosphere, views, the setting in the house – she felt inspired whenever she was in there – and deep-down, she knew it would make a calming and productive writing space.

But giving in to the idea would mean her decision had been made. And that decision was a leap she seemed incapable of making.

Pulling the zip further towards her chin, she settled back into the wicker chair, the woven threads creaking in the silent night air. Her eyes were drawn to the moon reflecting on the rippling waters. Both soothing and peaceful, it was a time of year she loved.

Funnily enough, watching the changing seasons had been one of the few things she'd missed when she'd first moved to London, the thought reminding her of never-ending pavements and concrete buildings that rolled on for miles. Occasionally, she and Darren had gone to Regent's Park or had taken the underground to Hyde Park, but that was as much countryside as she'd seen in the six years she'd been in London. Darren was a city boy through and through.

A flicker of light in the trees signalled a van approaching. Who on earth would be visiting at this time? she thought to herself.

She felt uneasy. There were no other houses on the road. She didn't get passing traffic: the dirt track was a dead end that stopped at Lochside.

Few people knew she was there. Abigail knew that her imagination could get carried away with itself, but this time, she felt her unease was justified and grabbed her mobile phone from the table.

Blinded by the headlights, she watched as the van parked. The engine fell silent, and the driver's door opened.

'Oh, Jamie, you scared me.' Abigail almost knocked her wine glass from the table as she rushed down the steps to meet him.

'Sorry, didn't mean to. I just wondered if you fancied some company?'

'Sure, but weren't you on a hot date?'

'Ah, well I was, but as you can tell, it didn't go so well.'

'What happened?'

'I think she got one of those it's-an-emergency calls,' he replied, shrugging his shoulders and making an *I'm fine* face that didn't fool Abigail.

'Oh, Jamie. I'm so sorry.' Abigail was surprised. She imagined that if you were looking for someone, Jamie would be quite the catch. He was funny, kind without taking any nonsense, and you could tell he'd been in the army, something about the way he carried himself.

Abigail wasn't entirely oblivious to his looks, either. He could be serious, but he had an engaging smile that caused his eyes to wrinkle at the corners, softening his features. His sandy blond hair and brown eyes complemented his chiselled jawline. And, at another time, he might have even been her type.

'Yeah, well, we didn't make it through the main course, and dessert's the best bit,' he joked.

But Abigail could see through his attempt at humour. Jamie was usually confident enough to brush things off as other people's issues, but she could see he was hurt. She knew enough to know he hadn't been overly keen, that Claire had done the chasing, had asked him out. But for her to then flee the date early was cruel. 'Glass of wine, coffee?'

'Coffee would be good, thanks. Decaf, if you've got it.'

They spent the next couple of hours chatting on the porch, Abigail in her grandmother's old armchair and Jamie sitting on a cushion as he leaned back against one of the porch's supporting posts.

At some point, Abigail had opened a box of her favourite chocolates as a treat since Jamie had missed out on dessert. And between them, they put the world to rights before discussing her plans for the house over the next couple of weeks.

Abigail was excited to get the new bathroom suite and kitchen installed. She was sure she'd feel she'd broken the back of the work by then.

'What happened to Mr Mackay? He was supposed to

be keeping on top of the garden and the house. He was to be getting paid from my grandmother's estate?'

'He died not long after you left.'

'Died?' A shiver spread across Abigail, its tentacles reaching her every limb. While a heat rose from the pit of her stomach causing her cheeks to flush, her thoughts turned to the markings on the carpet when she'd first opened the door, the day she'd arrived back at Lochside.

Someone had been in the house. She was sure of it. But who? Or had the marking simply remained from when Mr Mackay paid his last visit? No, definitely not, she told herself. The house wasn't dusty when she left it six years ago. The intruder had to have been recent.

'I'm sorry, Abigail. Did you know him well?' Jamie interrupted.

Composing herself, she decided to keep shtum, until she could be sure. 'No! How could I possibly know anyone from around here when I was never allowed to leave? The furthest I was ever allowed to go was up the track to the first corner, then I had to turn and come back.'

'Abigail, do you not remember anything?'

'Like what?' Her voice was quiet.

'About why you never left here.' Jamie gestured towards the surrounding landscape.

'N-no, why? Is there something I should know?' she asked, jumping to her feet and leaning against the handrail. Forcing straggly wisps of hair from her face as she went.

'Give it time. You'll remember when the time is right,'

Jamie replied, getting to his feet, and putting his hand on hers.

'What the hell kind of answer's that?' She pulled her hand away and walked towards the steps.

'The right one, trust me.' He caught up with her. 'You do trust me, don't you?'

She did trust him. Their friendship had ignited from the moment he first came in for a coffee and Abigail felt as though she'd known him for years. Even if her brain did seem determined to forget him.

Pulling her hands within her sleeves, she shivered in the cool night air.

'I'd better head. You still want me to pick up the old sofa tomorrow?'

'Yes, please. Where are you taking it?'

'It's just fit for the skip. You can come and help if you like. We could get a carry-out from Miranda's and bring it back here. Then I'll help you strip the last of the wallpaper, unless you desperately want to do it all yourself?' he joked.

'Ugh, would you? That would be great. I'm sick of the sight of it. It's just the old sewing room that's still to be stripped.'

'No problem. I'll see you about ten then?'

Abigail nodded and followed him towards his van. 'Jamie?'

'Yup.'

'The memories—'

He cut her off. 'Don't worry about those. They'll appear when you're good and ready.'

'But how did you know? You said when we first met that I'd blotted stuff out. How did you know about that?'

92

He took a step closer. She was shivering in the cool breeze, and he pulled her collar up around her neck, framing her auburn hair. She looked at him, her blue eyes pleading for an answer. 'Because I'm a part of those memories. But it's okay, they'll come back when you're ready.'

There was a flicker in his eyes. Did he want to say more? Part of her felt she should have prodded, asked more questions, but a bigger part of her was transfixed in the moment. His face was just inches from hers. His warm breath caressed her cheek, his eyes delving deep into hers. She felt safe.

'I'll see you in the morning.'

She stayed silent. His hands caressed the outsides of her arms, as though to protect her from the night air. Suddenly aware of her body, she felt a need from within.

She was lost in an all-consuming desire to have him, and confusion, as she tried to interpret what was happening between them.

'So...I'll see you in the morning.'

'Eh, yeah, see you in the morning' was all she could manage. She'd no idea what else he'd said. She could only watch as he walked to his van.

Abigail kept watching until his brake lights disappeared into the distance. She turned to gather up the empty glass and mug. Relieved to get into the warmth, she tried not to care that every sound she made echoed through the house, as if its sole purpose was to remind her she was alone.

Chapter Eleven

A new day and new dawn saw Abigail in her grandmother's sewing room. Having faced off against the same red and white roses on a sage-green background in the hall, Abigail was all too aware of how difficult the walls were going to be to strip.

But she knew that if she could have at least one wall done before Jamie arrived, it would be a head start on the day.

She steamed and scraped and re-steamed as the stubborn blasts of colour fought to stay put. By the time Jamie arrived, she had half of the wall with the doorway stripped and another broken nail, making a final tally of ten. At least there were no more to break, she consoled herself, scraping the sage-green dye from her fingertips.

Between them, it took two trips to the skip over a couple of hours. It wasn't so much the sofa that was the issue, but the numerous bags of wallpaper remnants. So, it was a relief for them both when they started on the final load.

There were also a couple of boxes for the charity shop, but these were filled with bits and pieces that belonged to Abigail from her time with Darren, things she no longer wanted to lie around.

'Come on then, slow coach,' Jamie joked. 'One last trip and then I'll treat you to lunch.'

'You don't have to do that. It's the shop's van. I'll pay.'

'No! This one's on me. Look at the place. Look what you've done already. And I'm guessing taking that lot to the charity shop is a bit of a milestone too. No, today's on me.'

Abigail could sense she wasn't going to win this one and thanked him as he drove up the dirt track towards the main road.

She couldn't help but revel in the scenery as Jamie turned off at Dunvegan and drove towards Portree. It was a journey she loved. The rolling hills that eventually led to the Quiraing had a way of putting her at ease. It was all beginning to feel like home. It felt familiar. Felt safe.

These feelings were reinforced as they drove into Portree. At that moment, she knew that if she did decide to sell Lochside and return to London, leaving Jamie and the island behind would be heart-wrenching. In more ways than one.

Having paid their last visit to the skip, Jamie waited for Abigail as she took her unwanted possessions from her life with Darren into the charity shop.

A symbolic moment that made her feel stronger. As though

a line had been drawn under her relationship with Darren, and she was officially moving on with her life. Wherever that life may be.

'Hi, you two. What can I get you today?' was the greeting that met them as they stepped into Miranda's.

Abigail and Jamie gave their orders to go and waited patiently while one of the café assistants began putting it all together. Abigail had got to know Miranda quite well over the last couple of months. Miranda was a few years older than her, but they had a similar sense of humour and often chatted when the café was quiet.

Today, though, it was busy. There was the usual Saturday buzz about the picturesque little town and, in typical Abigail fashion, she stared out of the window watching the world go by. The main road that ran past the café was a constant stream of traffic: a mixture of locals and tour buses embroiled in a who-can-hold-up-who-the-most situation.

The crossing was in continuous use as tourists from a varied assortment of buses poured onto the streets of Portree, causing a continuous battle between traffic and pedestrians.

Jamie had turned to read the noticeboard when Abigail spotted a middle-aged man zigzagging his way through said tourists on the other side of the street.

She squinted and, without taking her eyes off him for a second, grabbed Jamie's arm.

'Jamie, Jamie. Do you know him?' Her finger guided him through the crowds.

'Eh, no, don't think so.'

'Look closely. It's important.'

'Why, who is he?'

Still clutching his arm, she opened the door and dragged him out onto the pavement, nestling them among a group of tourists who were reading Miranda's menu board just outside the door.

'What are you doing?'

'Shh, just be calm. Have a good look.'

Abigail turned her back towards the middle-aged man but could make out his reflection in the café window. He was at the pedestrian crossing. She waited until the lights changed and watched as he crossed the street before turning to walk towards them. Giving Jamie a little nudge to ensure he was still paying attention, she watched the man's reflections as he strode purposefully past the café. She recognised the backpack as the one he'd had with him on the train: it was her American Tourist.

Still holding onto Jamie's arm, she turned to follow. He stopped at the small Co-op by the waterfront, where he stocked up on an excessive amount of bung-in-the-microwave meals. Then they followed him to the roundabout that brought everyone together as they drove into Portree, and up towards the industrial estate and the quieter end of town. Abigail noticed he kept his head down, never appearing to smile or say hello to anyone he passed.

He eventually led them to a warehouse on the edge of the industrial estate. Abigail tugged at Jamie's sleeve, pulling him into a doorway.

They watched, hidden from sight, as the American Tourist looked over both shoulders before entering a grey door.

'What the hell was all that about?' Jamie straightened the sleeve of his summer zip-up.

'I don't know, but he's up to no good.'

'What? I don't mean him. I mean you! And what do you mean, *He's up to no good*? The poor bloke only crossed the road and walked through town.'

Abigail told Jamie about her strange encounter on the train the night she arrived. He agreed it was odd but thought it could probably be easily explained.

'No, no. There's got to be more to it. Trust me, I'm usually right about these things. Well, apart from with Darren,' she muttered under her breath, before turning her attention back to the building.

She absorbed every inch of the nondescript structure that sat alongside local businesses, frantically searching for a hint as to what it was used for or who it belonged to. But, nothing. 'It's odd to have a warehouse with no business name outside. Don't you think?'

'Hmm, I don't know. The way he looked around before he went in, though. That was odd, I'll give you that much,' Jamie said.

An hour later and Abigail and Jamie had picked up their lunch and were sitting on her porch munching their way through a mixture of tuna mayo and ham salad sandwiches and, today's special, strawberry tarts.

'Oh, I swear, the best thing about this place is Miranda's baking.'

'Oh, gee, thanks very much.' Jamie raised his eyebrows while licking the last of the strawberry sauce from his fingers.

Abigail laughed. 'You okay? After last night, I mean.'

'Yeah, her loss.' But his expression wasn't convincing. 'Come on, let's get the last of this wallpaper off and then we can celebrate with a glass of red. What do you say?'

'Sounds good to me.'

They put a playlist on in the background and set to work. They'd lost more of the day than they'd anticipated between queues at the skip and their unplanned walk to the industrial estate. But they stuck at it and, as evening came and went and their stomach's rumbled a need for sustenance, they'd almost finished the last wall. Hoping they had their timings right, they stopped to order Chinese food.

They were both scrubbing at their sage-green fingertips when their meal arrived.

'Two carry-outs in one day. You're leading me astray,' Jamie joked. 'You could've at least cooked me a steak.'

Abigail chuckled. 'I'm not sure you'd want to eat it if I cooked it.'

'Really, you that bad?'

'Oh, worse, much worse!'

'Thank goodness for Chinese then.' He grinned, handing her the promised glass of red.

She joined him at the table. The light from the moon shone in through the curtainless window, illuminating his rugged good looks. For the second time in less than twenty-four hours, she felt something. Something more than friendship. Aware her eyes had been drawn to his mouth, she realised she was staring.

Flustered, she averted her eyes while, at the same time, realising she was always comfortable in his company. Always content. 'Cheers,' she managed, clinking her glass against his. 'And thank you so much for all your help today.'

'You're welcome.' He smiled, his eyes lingering on hers long enough for her to suspect there was a possibility he felt the same. 'We should go out for a meal tomorrow night. Celebrate our hard work—' His phone buzzed. The moment had gone. 'Oh, that's Claire.' Looking confused, he wandered into the hall.

Abigail picked at her Chinese. She was trying to be polite and wait for Jamie to return, but at the same time, she was starving. Moments later, he reappeared, sporting a grin that made Abigail's stomach lurch.

'Well, turns out it wasn't a fake it's-an-emergency-get-me-out-of-here call. It was an emergency. Her mum had taken unwell, low blood sugar or something, but she's fine now. I'm seeing her tomorrow night.'

'Oh, that's great, Jamie. That's great. I know you liked her, so-so…That's great. Yes, that's-that's great.' She realised she was rambling, stumbling over her words. She needed to stop talking, and quickly, before anything else fell incoherently from her mouth.

There was no denying Abigail was feeling something in the pit of her stomach. An ache. It confused her; she hadn't felt this way with Darren. Not at all. This was different and unexpected.

Chapter Twelve

'Jamie, are you sure you're going about this in the right way? Maybe you should tell Abigail how you feel. I mean, that's got to be better than continuing a relationship with a woman you're not interested in.'

'But Abigail's not interested in me, Mum. Not anymore. And it's time I faced the fact that she probably never will be. If anything, we're going to end up stuck in the friend zone because that's what she's needed since she returned. It's what she still needs, and anyway'—he sighed, running his fingers through his hair—'it's how she sees me.'

Glancing towards the mantelpiece and the photo of Abigail, he said, 'I've spent six horrendous years waiting, and now she's back. But she still can't remember us. Her memories are just as lost as they were when she left. I can't sit back and wait, not any longer. It's too painful. It's-it's time I moved on. Time I made a life for myself.'

'And do you think you can do that?

'I have no option. Not if I want to stay on the island.'

'You do, don't you? You want to stay on the island?'

'Yes. Yes, of course I do.'

His mum wrapped her arms around him, hugging him as though he were a young child who'd fallen out with his friends.

'Then stay, but don't write Abigail off just yet. Please, son. It's still early days.'

Chapter Thirteen

Abigail couldn't help but smile as she admired her kitchen. It was sleek, elegant, and fresh, everything her grandmother's wasn't. She'd opted for off-white doors with dark wooden worktops to match the old farmhouse table.

She'd had the windows replaced, a breakfast bar added to separate the kitchen and dining area, and had ordered a couple of stools in the same metal as the door handles.

The Belfast sink and solid wood shelving added a homely feel. Abigail was bursting to get into town. She could imagine a few plants dotted around and maybe a cookbook or two wouldn't hurt. You're never too old to learn, she decided.

Hearing her front door open, she hurried to thank Greg, the tiler. He was just loading his van, having put the finishing touches to her bathroom.

She'd got to know him quite well over the past couple of weeks as he'd been back and forth working around other tradesmen, getting both her bathroom and kitchen finished in time for the painter arriving tomorrow. The walls had already been skimmed and Abigail had chosen the colours.

She was itching to show Jamie, but she was sure he was out with Claire. They hadn't seen as much of each other recently, but he still called in if he was going into town and he was always texting, making sure she was all right.

Abigail grabbed a glass of wine and her laptop; some celebratory online shopping was in order. She thought about her bathroom: an elegant white suite with the sink set in a traditional blue vanity unit. White and blue patterned floor tiles were laid against a backdrop of gloss white rectangular wall tiles, which Greg had fitted halfway up each wall and behind the shower cubicle. The top half of the walls, she'd decided, were to be painted pitch blue.

She scrolled through websites, eventually ordering towels and a white chair that she thought would sit elegantly in the corner.

Having topped up her glass, she returned to her laptop. She knew she had to order a writing desk for her grandmother's old sewing room. Nothing fancy; something neutral that could be taken elsewhere when she finally made the all-important decision on her future. She thought about her brand-new kitchen and bathroom. All they'd done was to make it even harder for her to leave.

Which then served only to remind her about Jamie, about

staying at Lochside, and whether she would want to if he was to end up with Claire long term.

But her thoughts caught her off guard. Once again, she pushed them to the back of her mind, just as she'd learned to do with her unwanted childhood memories, forcing herself instead to search for a desk.

The more she searched, the more she could imagine the room finished. Her thoughts then turned to bookcases and somewhere for her printer. Before she knew it, an hour and a half had passed, and her orders had been confirmed.

Deciding some fresh air was in order, she wandered out to the porch and down towards the water. It was almost 8.00 p.m., and as August tipped into September, the sun was setting.

Watching the sun set from the jetty had become a habit. One day, if she decided to stay, she could imagine sitting at the end of the jetty in the old wicker chair, just as her grandmother had done. For the moment, the fragile jetty teetering precariously over the illuminated water was spectacular as the waves reflected the pinks and golds from the sky above. Her grandmother's little patch of the loch, the place Abigail had hated, was in danger of becoming her sanctuary.

As the tide progressed inwards, a heron that appeared to have taken up permanent residence at Lochside was fishing just a few metres along the shore.

She ventured onto the rickety old jetty and sat with her legs dangling over the water, just far enough out that she could clamber back to shore if it were to give way.

And it wasn't long before she was lost in the same old

quandary. Should she stay, or should she go? Where did her future lie? And, thanks to two glasses of red, it wasn't long before she was singing The Clash again, only this time out loud!

'Well, I think you should stay.'

Mortified, Abigail swung around to see Greg stepping onto the jetty. She was more than aware of the racket she'd just made; singing was not her forte. 'Sorry, I-I didn't hear your car.'

'Ha ha. I'm not surprised.'

Hiding her face in her cupped hands, she squirmed while Greg continued to laugh.

'May I join you?'

She could only nod.

Making his way along the jetty a little more gracefully than Abigail usually managed, he sat beside her, his legs long enough to rest on the rocks below. 'Nice evening, huh?'

'It is,' she agreed. Abigail was confused. She didn't know Greg socially, and she was sure he was finished working on the house. 'Is there a problem with the tiling?' she enquired, all the time thinking it must be about nine by now, surely far too late to be visiting a client about tiles!

'No, no. I, eh…I saw Jamie in town this afternoon. He was with someone else, and I realised that you two weren't a couple.' His face flushed a little, his eyes looking everywhere except at her. 'So, I was wondering if you would like to go for dinner sometime…with me?'

Abigail was taken aback. Greg was good-looking, tall,

with dark-brown hair, and she'd noticed he'd scrubbed up well as soon as she'd seen him standing at the end of the jetty. But, not once in all the time that he'd been working at the house had she thought of him in any way other than as a tiler.

She thought about Jamie: his smile, and the way he made her feel. But she was sure he was smitten with Claire, and she was not the type of person to come between another couple.

She knew she had to keep her feelings for Jamie in check or risk losing his friendship, and that was something she couldn't bear.

She was also aware that Jamie was currently her only form of social life. 'Yeah, that would be nice,' she said, her words more an automatic response than a desire.

'Great.' The relief was obvious in his expression. 'How about tomorrow? There's a place I know that looks over the Quiraing. The Pine Lodge Hotel. I could pick you up around seven thirty?'

'Okay, sounds good.'

'Great, see you then.'

Abigail watched as Greg rose from the jetty and headed towards his car. She returned his wave and noticed his broad smile. He was good-looking, well-built, and she knew from their conversations that he had a sense of humour, was into sports, jogged, and worked out.

They'd often chatted over a mug of coffee while he worked at her house and, in her obvious naivety, Abigail had thought nothing of it. Presumably, she decided, because she always thought of Jamie as the man in her life. But he wasn't. They were friends, close friends, and nothing more. And, given he'd started going out with Claire after Abigail had arrived back at Lochside, it was obvious – whether she liked it or not. He had no interest in her romantically.

Chapter Fourteen

The next evening, Abigail opted for a sleeveless floral dress she'd bought not long before she'd left London. Fitted at the waist and sitting a couple of inches above her knees, it flattered her slim build and long legs. The pale pastel colours set on a green background complemented her dark, auburn hair and she picked out a pale cropped denim jacket to stave off any chill later.

She was, however, realising that she was more excited about having a chance to dress up than she was about going on a date with Greg. She kept telling herself she might be pleasantly surprised. After all, she didn't really know him.

Greg arrived on time, still sporting his broad grin from yesterday. Abigail could tell he was far more invested in the evening than she was, but she was determined to give him a chance.

Thanking him as he opened her door, she couldn't help but watch as he made his way around to his side of the car. The more she studied him, the more she realised how attractive he was, and she wondered how she hadn't spotted this while he'd been coming and going over the last few weeks.

To her relief, they didn't struggle for conversation. Instead, they chatted all the way to the hotel. Once parked, Greg hurried around and opened her door.

'Thank you, but you don't have to do that, you know.'

'I'm trying my best to impress,' he joked, leading her towards the main door.

The hotel was elegant, stylish, and nestled on the edge of the cliffs that led down to the sea. Abigail took in the stunning, panoramic views of the Quiraing, before turning to look back at the silvery waters and the Scottish mainland in the distance.

She presumed it was an old estate house that'd been given a new lease of life. And as she entered the foyer, she couldn't help but admire the ornate carvings alluding to a grander past.

Greg held open the solid wooden door that led to the restaurant. It was busy, but the tables were spread out in a way that meant it wasn't in the least bit noisy. An imposing open fireplace with a mantel dominated the room, and Abigail imagined it would be beautiful when lit.

A waiter led them to their window table. The sun was about to set behind the Quiraing, and the sea had taken on a variety of muted tones that only added to the evening's serenity.

'Wow, what a view. It's lovely here.'

'I'm glad you like it. There are some nice walks around here too. A lot of people come for a walk through the Quiraing and then here for lunch. It's always a bit fancier at night, though.'

Their waiter brought the wine list, and once drinks were ordered they perused their menus. Pan-fried scallops with pancetta were the starter of choice for both of them, with Abigail opting for a loin of lamb for her main course and Greg, a steak.

Once their order was taken, Abigail could sense Greg was beginning to relax. They chatted about their day, about Greg's work and how he was hoping to branch out, maybe take on an apprentice, which raised his next question.

'So, Abigail, do you work? I mean, I'm presuming it's from home, given you were always there when I was in working.'

'Yes, I'm an author.'

'Cool, have you written anything I'd have read?'

'I doubt they'd be your thing. I write novels. I have one coming out this month.'

She'd been trying not to think about it. She knew Joanna was expecting her to return to London for the launch and Abigail could think of nothing worse. Although, at this late stage, she knew she didn't have a choice.

The rest of the evening passed pleasantly. There had been no lulls in conversation, and Abigail liked Greg. *Liked* being the operative word, as she was aware she wasn't desperately hoping for another date.

She couldn't understand why. He'd been nothing but a gentleman, funny, and kind. And he did have the loveliest eyes, which Abigail had spent most of the evening admiring silently.

But, for her, there was undoubtedly no spark.

She had the impression that it was quite the opposite for Greg. He'd casually slipped into the conversation the Hollywood blockbuster that was showing at the cinema next week. He'd casually mentioned Friday, and Abigail had casually nodded along.

Greg brought his car to a halt outside Lochside and, once again, hurried around to open her door. Abigail was aware, as they strolled towards the porch, that the polite thing to do would be to offer him a coffee but, until she sorted out her feelings, she didn't want to lead him on.

Now gone eleven, the island air was giving way to a chilly ocean breeze. As Abigail pulled her denim jacket closed, Greg leaned in to help. Ever attentive, ever the gentleman.

They walked up the steps together, the first awkward silence of the evening deafening as their eyes locked.

'Thank you for coming out tonight, Abigail. I've had a really good time.'

'So have I.' She wasn't lying. She had, but…

'Can I see you again? Maybe we could go to the cinema on Friday like I said. If you're free?'

'Yes. Yes, that would be nice.' The words were out as if she were running on autopilot. She needed to be alone, to gather her thoughts. She knew she would have been more than happy to give Greg a second glance back in the city and would've been thrilled if he'd asked her out.

She needed to work out why she was having a lovely time

with him but wasn't excited by it. 'Well, it's getting cold.' She tilted her head towards the door.

He nodded. 'Friday, then. Pick you up at seven?'

'Perfect.'

Then there it was: that awkward moment. Greg looked down at her lips and then at her cheek. She could tell he was wondering what he should do. The lips, the cheek, or not at all?

Abigail stood, frozen in embarrassment, while Greg leaned forward. She had no idea where he was going, but eventually, his lips caressed hers. Just lightly but enough to ignite something. Suddenly, he had her full attention!

There must have been something in her eyes because Greg smiled, looked relieved, and leaned in for a longer, more passionate kiss. His lips had awakened hers and she responded, her hand reaching up and cupping his cheek. Greg received exactly the reaction he'd hoped for, and Abigail had no idea where it'd come from.

Chapter Fifteen

The next few days flew by as Abigail oversaw work on the house. Fortunately, as each job had progressed, there had been no unexpected discoveries so, apart from the inevitable upheaval, it'd all gone to plan.

Pete, the painter Jamie had recommended, was keeping to his schedule, and both the living room and Abigail's writing room were finished. He'd just started the largest bedroom and Abigail was eagerly awaiting the arrival of two new sofas and a matching chair.

Meanwhile, her desk and bookcase had arrived. Conveniently flat packed, the pieces to the desk were spread across her old bedroom floor. Normally, she would've hated coming into this room but, as the house was transforming, she was beginning to feel more at ease within its walls and was even contemplating taking her grandmother's old bedroom; it made far more sense given it was the biggest.

Once again, she was so engrossed in her thoughts that she hadn't heard the front door opening.

'Hello, Abigail. You here?'

She flinched. I've got to stop doing that, she thought as Jamie wandered in.

'There you are. You look like you're having fun.' He grinned.

Abigail jumped to her feet. The next thing she knew she had her arms wrapped around his neck.

'Hey. You okay?'

She nodded but didn't let go. She was realising just how much she'd missed him.

Jamie held her for a few moments, seeming to sense something was up.

Composing herself, she pulled back. 'Do you have time for a coffee?'

'Yeah, I've got all afternoon if you need a hand with this lot.'

'Really, that would be great!' It wasn't so much that she was unable to build a desk; she was more than capable. It was more that she'd missed having him around and could do with his company. Her fifty-something painter was efficient and a perfectionist, but there was no chat, not even a coffee stop.

'Is everything okay?' he asked, following her into the kitchen.

'Yeah.'

'Come on, it's me you're talking to. I don't believe you.'

Abigail filled the kettle and put it on to boil before nodding towards her laptop, which was lying open on the kitchen table. Clicking on the most recent email from Joanna, she turned the laptop to face him.

Jamie took a seat. It was the full itinerary for her book launch events in London.

'Normally there would be far more events, but Joanna's only booked in a select few. She's chosen the ones with larger profiles, that'll create more of an impact.'

Jamie let out a sigh. 'Do you have to go through with all this?'

'Yeah, I kind of have to.'

'I mean it's great from the point of view of your writing, but I'm guessing you're not ready to go back to London just yet.'

Abigail could feel her eyes brimming up.

Jamie rose from his chair and wrapped his arms around her. 'Oh, here, come on. This is going to be great for your novel. You've got to think about it that way. It's a week in London, and, as Joanna said, she's condensed it as much as possible for you.'

'I know, and it's weird. I don't understand why I feel like this. I've been struggling to decide whether I want to stay here permanently or sell up, and then here I am faced with a week away, and I don't want to leave.'

'Will Darren play any part in this?'

She thought back over the heart-to-hearts she'd had with Jamie since returning to Lochside. 'No…No, but it'll be all over social media, so he'll know I'm around.'

'Where will you stay?'

'Joanna tried to insist I stay with her, but I've booked a hotel. She has a house full of young kids and enough on her plate.' Abigail pulled away as the kettle reached its boil.

After a few moments of silence, Jamie spoke again. 'How about I come with you?'

'What?' She said, almost missing his mug as she added milk, 'W-well, can you? I mean, will Claire not mind?'

'No, she'll be fine. Anyway, she knows we go way back.'

'Apparently!' She threw him a look.

He rolled his eyes. 'Well, I'd say you are probably one of my closest friends and you've only been back on the island a few months. I'll worry about you back there. Not because you can't cope but because having a friend with you might just let you relax enough to enjoy your achievement. You've earned this, Abigail. You're a bloody good writer and you deserve to go.'

He grabbed his mug and took a sip. 'Think about it. The offer's there. Now, you got any biscuits? I'm starving.'

Laughing through happy tears, Abigail handed him a packet of KitKats. 'It would be great if you could come. But please, make sure Claire is okay with it first. I don't want to cause you any trouble there.'

'Oh, she'll be fine! She's quite laid back, a bit too laid back at times.'

'Oh?' Abigail sensed a tone.

'Yeah, we're just different that way. She isn't as vocal or demonstrative as me about things or about how she feels.'

'Is everything okay?'

'Yeah, yeah, I think so.'

'Do you see yourself with her long term?'

'Erm, I think so.'

Abigail knew him well enough to know he wasn't being honest, and she couldn't help but wonder if he was doubting his own feelings, or Claire's. In the end, she reluctantly presumed it was Claire's, given he was complaining about not knowing how she felt.

The next couple of hours were spent deciphering the wad of instructions that typically accompanied flat-packed furniture and then building the desk and bookcases.

There was laughter, a lot of laughter, and a little frustration at the lack of content to some of the instructions. But any frustrations were quickly followed by a sense of achievement when they placed the various pieces into their designated spots in Abigail's new writing room.

Excitedly, Abigail hurried to the kitchen and grabbed a chair. And, as if savouring the moment, she placed it in front of her desk before slowly lowering herself into position.

She could see as far up the driveway as was possible before the road snaked off to the left. The sparse wood, which separated the road from the loch to her right and the rolling hills to her left, dappled the uneven dirt track in the late afternoon sun. And her jetty, looking elderly and fragile, teetered above the glistening water.

'Oh, this is perfect. Perfect. Perfect.' For the first time, since she'd arrived at Lochside, plot lines and character descriptions were bursting to the fore, and she found herself desperately wanting to write.

A feeling of calm, of being herself, of relief, finally washed over her as she soaked in the views, atmosphere, and the invaluable feeling of having a purpose again.

'Right, come on then. You owe me dinner!' Jamie announced, rubbing his hands together. 'Grab your coat.'

'Wh-where are we going?'

'You'll see. Just bring a jacket that'll keep out the wind.'

Abigail grabbed her jacket and bag and followed Jamie to his van. Usually, once they'd turned left at the end of her road, they would swing right after a few miles and go cross-country to Portree. But this time, Jamie continued straight ahead.

'Where are we going?'

'You're taking me for some fine dining.'

Abigail frantically tried to read his expression. Worried he was serious, she looked down at her outfit. Old skinny jeans with ripped knees and a T-shirt that bore the words *In my defence, they left me unsupervised* weren't quite suited to a fancy establishment.

In the end, she concluded that fine dining wasn't really Jamie's thing and so decided to play along with whatever he was up to.

A few more miles and they entered a village. The village Abigail had heard about but had never seen.

Searching for a sliver of familiarity, a memory, an image, anything, Abigail studied her surroundings. A butcher's, a baker's-cum-fish and chip shop, and a small grocery store that boasted Jamie's family's surname sat neatly in a row. A quaint café-cum-indie gift shop was nestled snuggly beside a small hotel further down the street. And all had open views out to the North Atlantic Ocean.

Not surprisingly, given the view, the remainder of the main street was a mixture of homes and guest houses. Her eyes absorbed the picturesque village. Low stone walls and fences surrounded many of the houses. Their gardens had succumbed to the island weather and appeared to have been given over to roaming sheep: a feature she quite liked on the island.

But nothing was familiar. Instead, feelings of being hidden away during her childhood were once again brought to the fore. How could she not have known all of this was here?

The next thing she knew, they were pulling up outside his parents' grocery store. 'Come on. You can pick the burgers.' And with that, he was running into the shop.

Abigail followed, confused but at the same time intrigued. It seemed to stock everything from everyday essentials to pet and farm goods. There was even a small section of outdoor clothing.

She found Jamie hunting in the fridge aisle for coleslaw.

'What on earth are you doing?'

'You grab the burgers, whatever type you like.'

Still wondering what on earth he had planned, she teasingly shrugged her shoulders and headed towards the meat section. Scanning the various options, she settled on a pack of four steak-and-onion burgers before searching the aisles once again. This time she found Jamie balancing all sorts in his arms. Shaking her head jokingly, she came to his rescue with a basket.

'You idiot,' she managed through her laughter. 'Put those in here.' And with the basket full, he was off again, only to return moments later with Abigail's favourite bottle of red.

'Hello, Abi.' The calm, cautious voice took her by surprise as a woman in her late fifties walked towards her.

'Hello.'

Jamie looked uneasy. 'This, eh, this is my mum, Morag. You probably won't remember her.'

'Let her have a look for herself,' his mum scolded, as if he were still a child. 'You never know, eh, love?' she said, smiling at Abigail. 'Memory can fool around with us sometimes.'

Abigail perused every inch of Morag Campbell's face, but nothing. 'I'm sorry, have we met?'

'Oh, yes, love. We have. But it was several years ago.'

'Well, it's lovely to meet you again.' Abigail smiled. 'And the village is beautiful. I can't believe I don't remember it.'

Morag's gaze momentarily darted towards Jamie. 'Well, it's been a while I suppose, but it's nice to see you back on the island again, my dear. And remember, if you need anything, anything at all, we're always here.'

Thanking Morag, she helped Jamie ferry their purchases back to the van. 'Your mum was hoping I'd recognise her, wasn't she?'

Jamie gave her an apologetic smile.

'I knew her, didn't I?'

'Yeah, you did. You both got on well, actually. But it's okay. She understands.'

Abigail scrutinised every inch of countryside as the road snaked between shoreline to one side and rolling hills to the other. It was beautiful, and for the life of her, she couldn't understand why she was unable to remember it from her childhood. Surely, she would've had to travel this road with her grandmother at some point. Unless, of course, her grandmother travelled it alone!

'Here we are!'

'Where? Where are we?'

'My boatyard! I wanted you to be the first to see it now that it's officially mine and has been cleared out a bit.'

'Is this why I've hardly seen you?'

'Yup, sorry. But you are its first visitor if that's any consolation.'

'You-you haven't brought Claire to see it?'

'Oh, god. No, she'd hate it!' he exclaimed, exiting the van and leading the way. 'I thought we'd have a barbecue on the jetty. What do you say?'

'Yessss!' She grabbed her jacket. Her eyes swallowed the view. 'Jamie, it's stunning. It's a completely different view of the loch. I love it.'

His jetty was rather more spectacular than the old, rickety contraption she had back at Lochside. Its solid concrete ramp sloped into the loch as though it was part of the landscape.

She stood for a few minutes, soaking in the views before Jamie reappeared from one of the old sheds. He was pulling a barbecue and grinning like a Cheshire cat as he wheeled it onto the jetty.

It was made from an old beer keg, and it looked like he'd been itching for the chance to use it. Abigail could tell he was in his element as he lit the charcoals and opened the wine.

'It'll be a while heating up, but a glass to pass the time?' He held up the bottle of wine, teasingly.

'Yes, please.' Abigail held out a plastic cup that Jamie had brought from the shed.

'Sorry, I forgot about glasses.'

Abigail laughed. 'It'll still taste good.'

Jamie threw a couple of thick blankets that he had folded several times onto the jetty, and together they sat down, legs outstretched, eyes submerged in the loch's beauty.

'This is perfect, Jamie. Simply perfect.'

'You haven't tasted my cooking yet,' he joked.

'Will you come to the city with me, for the whole week?'

'I said I would, didn't I?'

'It certainly feels more appealing now that I'm not going alone. You'll have a lot of hanging around though. At the events, I mean.'

'Yeah, I figured as much but that's fine. Book another room at your hotel. I'll be your breakfast buddy, save you eating alone in among all the couples,' he joked.

'That reminds me. I was on a date the other night and I have another again tomorrow.'

'A-a date?'

'It's Greg, the tiler,' she continued.

'Greg...I, eh, I didn't see that coming. Do you like him?'

'Neither did I! I wasn't that fussed at first, but I'm looking forward to tomorrow.' She thought that covered the final part of his question without committing too much.

A few moments of silence passed before Jamie hit his

plastic cup against Abigail's. 'Oh well, here's to tomorrow then.'

It was always easy passing time with Jamie, and as she sat on the jetty, watching the ducks, the sailing boats, and the sun giving way to the evening, she was probably the most relaxed she'd been since she'd arrived at Lochside.

And Abigail had to hand it to Jamie: he did a mean barbecue. Her burger and trimmings were delicious, as was the surprise dessert. 'I'm presuming that having a love life hasn't affected your sweet tooth.'

Blushing, she chose a cupcake from the box Jamie had placed between them. 'What was Claire up to today?'

'She was in town with a friend. I'm seeing her Saturday.'

'I thought you two were joined at the hip?'

'On the contrary, I see her twice a week at most. I've probably seen you more than I've seen her, until lately, that is, while I've been clearing out the yard.'

'I'd no idea you'd been doing all this.'

'Yeah, I wanted to surprise you, get your honest reaction.'

That, right there: that was the moment everything made sense. She'd felt confused between Jamie and Greg, but now she could see that was purely because she didn't want to lose Jamie as a friend. Recently, she'd been worried she had. She'd presumed he'd been spending every minute he could with Claire, which would've been fair enough, and she knew that.

But at the same time, he had become one of her closest friends, and the thought of losing him had resulted in her feeling down and confused about Greg. She now knew that she and Jamie were fine. Their friendship was intact. Life was good.

Chapter Sixteen

Abigail waited as Greg bought their tickets. It'd been months since she was last at the cinema and, if she were being honest with herself, she still wasn't sure what excited her the most: a date with Greg or a night out.

It was clear that he, on the other hand, was under no illusions as to how he felt, and Abigail was aware that he was far more invested in building a relationship than she was. There was no denying she enjoyed his company and, as he tried to balance their extra-large sharing popcorn, two drinks, and tickets, she felt perhaps his chivalry was going a step too far.

'Please, let me carry something.'

'Thanks.' Greg, obviously flustered, turned a darker shade of red as she rescued their popcorn, which had been balancing precariously on the two drinks cups wedged in his left hand.

'Relax, I'm not one of these women who likes to have everything done for her. Come on'—she giggled, trying desperately to put him at ease—'we're on this date together.'

But no sooner were the words out of her mouth, than they were separated by a crowd of teenagers as they shoved their way through the organised queue, barging straight through the screening room doors that Abigail and Greg were heading towards.

By the time Abigail and Greg found each other again, his rugged good looks had returned to their normal shade of pale.

'You okay?'

'Yeah.' She giggled.

'Look, I'm sorry. I'm nervous, I-I like you, and…'

'I know, and I like you too.' It wasn't a lie – she did like him – she just wasn't sure if she meant it in quite the same way as he did. But she did think it was worth persevering and finding out. She remembered how surprised she'd been when he kissed her. Maybe there was something there. Maybe it didn't always have to be a lightning bolt.

Reaching up, she kissed him on the cheek. 'Come on, lead the way.'

She knew instantly she'd put him at ease and, as they took their seats, she was relieved that their conversation turned to more relaxed chatter.

The evening flew by and, as Greg drove them back to her grandmother's house, Abigail tried to decide whether she should invite him in for a coffee. She still had to tell him she was returning to London for her book launch.

Although the launch itself wasn't the issue, she needed to find a way of telling him that Jamie would be coming with her, without giving him the wrong idea.

Greg pulled up outside her house and together they walked towards her decking. He took her hand. 'I'd a really good time tonight.'

'So did I.'

'You free Sunday? We could go for a walk. Get some lunch, maybe?'

Oh, well. Here goes, she thought to herself. There was, after all, only one response. 'I can't. I'm going back to London, for my book launch. I leave Sunday morning and I'll be away for the week.'

'Oh, okay.' She could see in his eyes he was disappointed, but his smile let her know he was happy for her. 'It's amazing what you do. I'll have to read it.' His hands were gliding up and down the outsides of her arms. She couldn't decide if it was to reaffirm his regard for her work or to help stave off the late-night chill.

'Oh, you don't have to. It's probably not your cup of tea, anyway.'

'I want to. I'll order it online and read it while you're away.'

Abigail smiled. She'd already received her author copies, but a second date felt far too soon to offer him one. 'Jamie is coming with me,' she blurted out.

Greg squinted, his hands recoiling from her arms. He had no idea of the circumstances that surrounded her leaving London, so she knew he wouldn't understand the need for Jamie's company.

'He offered to come. Purely for moral support, that's all.'

'Look, Abigail. It's up to you who you see and when. I'm- I'm just surprised, that's all.'

'Why don't you come in for a coffee? You deserve to know why he's coming, and I'll need a coffee to talk about it.'

She unlocked the door and, as Greg followed her to the kitchen, the change in his demeanour was obvious. He wasn't angry or upset; Abigail got the impression he was more worried. Worried that he perhaps had a rival and knew he'd lost.

Greg took a seat at the table while Abigail put the kettle on and grabbed two mugs from the cupboard above. There was an awkward silence as the kettle took its time. Abigail popped to the toilet, partly to kill time and partly to muster up the courage to talk about Darren.

When she returned, Greg handed her a mug. 'Hope you don't mind, I just got stuck in.'

'No, that's great,' she replied, warming her hands on the mug. 'I'm still waiting for the sofas to arrive, so we'll have to sit in here.'

She tried to sound upbeat as she nodded towards the kitchen table but, deep-down, the thought of talking about Darren was unbearable. And not because she was devastated, heartbroken, and missing him. Far from it. But because of the betrayal, the feeling of not being good enough, of being unloved, of being so naive and so unaware of what had been going on for so long. Of being so unimportant, yet again!

Greg listened as Abigail told him about her life in London, her relationship with Darren, and the weekend's events that'd led to her boarding the train for Lochside. She explained why Jamie had offered to accompany her and why his offer had made the trip bearable.

She explained how she'd spent so much of her time trying to decide whether she should stay permanently in her grandmother's house or whether she should sell it and make a fresh start somewhere else. But, as she did so, a feeling of clarity washed over her. It was as though the fog was lifting, and her decision had finally and unequivocally been made. She wanted to stay.

The thought of returning to London – even if only for a week – of leaving her writing room and its views across the water, of leaving the calmness and stillness she felt in a place she'd only ever related to as isolating: it was now gut-wrenching.

Abigail lifted her head, looking Greg in the eyes for the first time since they'd sat down. He'd been listening intently, showing he understood. Not only why she'd felt the way she had, but also why Jamie's company would make such a difference. It was a week which, after all, was a celebration of a successful writer who deserved to enjoy every minute of her trip.

Greg reached for her hand. He held it tightly in his. 'I'm so sorry, Abigail. You don't deserve to be treated like that, ever. And I didn't mean to make you talk about something so upsetting. I just wasn't sure of the situation between you and Jamie, that's all.'

'It's okay. I get why you might have been confused, and I've not exactly been open about what's gone on in my life, either.'

Though Abigail had to admit to herself she didn't have that

same desire to be with Greg that he clearly had to be with her. Her thoughts turned to Jamie: his relationship with Claire, and how he made her feel. But then she consoled herself with the fact that Greg had been the one to ask her out! He'd been the one who'd thought of her in that way, and she'd been the one taken by surprise. Maybe this is normal? she thought. Maybe this is what it feels like when you are the one being asked?

Suddenly aware of her silence, she said, 'Jamie and I are friends, good friends. And I know he didn't start going out with Claire until after I returned to the island. He doesn't think of me that way.'

She was aware she was saying all the right things. Saying what she knew she should say. Saying what he wanted to hear. And it was all true, but to her, her feelings for Greg were a separate issue, one to which he seemed oblivious.

Studying his expression as he sipped his coffee, Abigail was certainly not oblivious to his rugged good looks or how his hair sat wildly around his face. Not in an untidy way, just maybe a bit unruly, as if it had a mind of its own.

And his eyes: she took a minute to find the right word. Enticing. They were enticing, she reiterated to herself, but with a playful glint that came and went. Quite a sexy glint, she decided.

She'd noticed the same look in his smile when he was completely relaxed. She got the impression he could be quite mischievous when he wasn't nervously wondering if there was another man at play.

Greg let go of her hand and sat forward. He was silent,

thoughtful, his elbows resting on the table, his hands now clasped together. And when he turned to face her, his expression was unusually serious. 'What about you? Do you have feelings for him?'

Surprised at the question, she locked her eyes with his. Had he just offered her a way out? Was it as simple as telling him she had feelings for Jamie? Would that make him leave? That, after all, would be a much kinder let-down than admitting she didn't have any feelings for him other than friendship.

But it didn't matter that her heart skipped a beat at the mere thought of Jamie. It didn't matter that she relished every minute she spent with him, or that she missed him when he wasn't around. He was with Claire.

Part of her wanted to stay quiet, to not open that particular rabbit hole, but she knew Greg deserved the truth. So, what was stopping her?

Her eyes fell to his broad shoulders, to his muscles, and to the sinews flexing in his neck as he nervously awaited her response. She let her glance travel along his jawline and up to his lips. Remembering how they'd made her feel, she yearned for him to kiss her once again, not understanding, for one second, why she hadn't noticed him in this way before.

She reached for his hand. Her blue eyes swam in a pool of hazel. Her lips parted invitingly as desire took hold. No words needed.

Greg gently brushed her hair from her eyes. The sexy glint she'd reflected on earlier had returned and was now focussed solely on her. His lips hesitated, just long enough to feed her desire, her need, her longing to be kissed, to be touched, to be loved. Surely this is what it's supposed to be like, she thought, her doubts washing away.

Chapter Seventeen

Abigail scanned the bookshop. Joanna was part way through her now well-rehearsed introduction and Jamie was at Abigail's side, his presence keeping her grounded as she attempted to stay calm.

Listening for her cue, her heart raced, its thudding echoing in her ears. They were already four days into events, but this was the one Abigail had been dreading. The one that had haunted her thoughts. The one that had overshadowed her entire week.

It was the reason she'd insisted on taking a taxi back to the hotel after lunch, to allow for a quick outfit change. She'd known that no matter how much bubbly was on offer, she would need to power dress to get herself through the afternoon's event.

Unusually for her, she'd opted for a stylish black tapered-leg jumpsuit with black slingback stilettos. She'd also taken the time to drag the straighteners through her hair and darken her lipstick to a deeper shade of red.

As soon as she'd reappeared in the foyer, Jamie had known something was up. And when she hadn't crumpled at his jokes, he'd begun to work out that this was the event that a certain someone might turn up to. He had, however, expected that certain someone to be Darren until Abigail had told him otherwise.

The events so far hadn't disappointed, and Joanna had been ecstatic at the turnout while Abigail had been delighted to catch up with booksellers and readers she'd come to know so well over the years.

She had tried to convince herself that this was just another event and, therefore, should be treated no differently, but her sweaty palms, dry mouth, and exploding chest were all coming to a different conclusion.

'...and so, without further ado, please welcome Abigail Sinclair.'

Abigail went to take a step forward, but her legs froze. Silhouetted by sunlight streaming through the stained-glass window of the charming old bookshop, a figure was unmistakable. Abigail watched as the figure sauntered confidently past the seating area, her arms laden with books.

'Abigail, Abigail, you're up.' Jamie nudged her, but as he followed her gaze, he clocked the figure who was now unloading her armful of books onto a shelf and registered the severity of the situation. 'Go, go, I'll deal with her.' He gave Abigail a much-needed shove in the necessary direction.

The next couple of hours flew past and Abigail had lost count of the number of books she'd signed and hands she'd shaken.

Joanna had been on top form, introducing Abigail to all manner of bookshop managers and publishing contacts she'd invited to the various events throughout the week. And, true to form, had crammed as many contacts as she could into Abigail's run of events.

If Abigail had thought for one moment she was getting off lightly with only a week-long stint, then she'd been very much mistaken.

To her relief, there had been no sign of Toothbrush Girl either, after Jamie had promised to *deal with her*.

Jokingly, Abigail had commented to Joanna that she hoped he hadn't done away with her altogether. But she'd later discovered that a quick comment from him about her shameless lack of empathy or humiliation for her actions, which were quite frankly abhorrent, had been enough to send her scurrying to the stockroom for the event's duration.

As the afternoon came to an end, Joanna thanked Abigail and the audience members for their time. But not before a well-placed teaser about how Abigail's latest manuscript had utterly captivated her and how she hoped she would see everyone again next year when it hit the shelves.

The audience's reaction was to burst into a round of applause and Jamie could only admire Abigail for her composure as she thanked everyone for coming.

Chapter Eighteen

At just past 7.00 p.m., Abigail introduced Jamie to Libby and Grace, all the while trying to dodge the teasing glances thrown in her direction as Libby and Grace's eyes inhaled every inch of Jamie's looks and stature.

Both were married, although that didn't always matter in Libby's case. She was the walking embodiment of *It's perfectly alright to window shop as long as you don't fondle the goods.*

'Where the hell is Georgia?' Still in work mode, Joanna checked her watch and craned her neck each time the door opened. 'Honestly, that girl wouldn't know time if it smacked her in the forehead. Six thirty. I told her to be here at six thirty. Sharp.'

'But we met at seven,' Jamie whispered.

'I know.' Abigail chuckled, refilling her glass. 'But you've to build in at least an extra half hour if you want Georgia to arrive on time. I think possibly she's rumbled us, though.'

Having reached the end of her week-long run of events, Abigail was revelling in the successes and opportunities it'd brought. And the sheer joy of spending time with her friends.

When Georgia finally arrived, Libby and Grace were in the depths of interrogating Jamie, stopping only to scold Abigail for not pouncing on him and claiming him as hers.

He was holding his own, though. Libby managed to keep to her mantra, just. And Grace, who was slightly suspicious of Abigail's feelings, was apprising Jamie of Abigail's many endearing qualities, just in case he hadn't noticed them for himself.

And Abigail was in her element as laughter followed laughter while they caught up on their news and revelled in the pure joy of an evening out together at Piquant.

At some point in the evening, Georgia had alerted them to the latest pickle she'd inadvertently found herself in and had listened intently as her friends had given their valued advice, yet again!

Joanna ensured the food and wine flowed as it should and Abigail simply enjoyed every minute of being back in her favourite restaurant, with the people she loved.

She graciously accepted her friends' comments as they showered her with praise and pride for her accomplishments. But she quickly moved the subject on. Tonight was about them being together. Her little posse of five and the man she knew she loved with every fibre of her being.

Chapter Nineteen

Abigail relaxed in her chair, satisfied at yet another chapter edited, and drank in the panoramic landscape.

The sparse wood that'd fought so stubbornly to survive in the North Atlantic weather, the loch, the rolling hills, the mountains in the distance, and the wildlife: it all came together to create a scene that she was becoming far more attached to than she'd thought possible.

And then there was her brand-new jetty, standing proudly, elegantly, and level, above the receding tide. To her surprise, Jamie had called in a couple of favours and had organised for the old one to be removed and a new one built in its place while they were in London. They'd apparently finished just in the nick of time too, only leaving Lochside within an hour of Jamie and Abigail returning.

It was T-shaped, just like the old jetty, but wider. There was now enough space at the end of the jetty for half a dozen chairs. Closing her eyes and smiling contentedly, she imagined sharing a few bottles with Joanna, Libby, Grace, Georgia, and Jamie as they laughed into the night. Oh, and Greg, she remembered, scolding herself for being such a bad human and dropping him from her thoughts, yet again.

It wasn't until she'd returned from London that she realised just how much the house and its surroundings had come to mean to her. She was taken aback at the relief she'd felt when she walked through the front door, into the house she'd transformed. The house that her grandmother would now barely recognise.

Despite years of feeling an abundance of isolation and heartache with her grandmother, Abigail now knew this was where she belonged.

Not a day had gone by since she'd returned from London that she hadn't been drawn to her writing room, to its views, and her keyboard. And each day, she'd aimed to write a few pages at least, although on days where she'd had no interruptions, she'd optimistically aimed for a couple of chapters. Anything more was a bonus.

Reaching for her empty coffee mug, she went to get a refill. But the sun radiating into the living room through the panoramic window lured her in instead. Her eyes danced around the room as she admired its recent transformation.

The new suite had finally arrived. The hideous floral relic her grandmother had loved so much had been replaced by two

Scandinavian-style pale-grey sofas, and an armchair that, most importantly, was luxuriously comfortable.

The pale-green and mustard cushions she'd scattered brightened the room, allowing the green of the woods to be drawn inside. The old, worn carpet had been replaced by light ash wooden flooring, which led to the kitchen.

The floral, claustrophobic theme that'd been so over-whelmingly oppressive, had now been replaced by a peaceful, airy atmosphere that Abigail had allowed to flow through the rest of the house.

The colour scheme continued up the hall. Stopping for a moment, she thought back to that dreadful day last April when she'd returned to Lochside. The dust, the lack of furniture, the floral walls and carpets, and the hideous sofa!

She remembered the spontaneous fits of coughing that'd continued to irritate her chest and nose as she'd hoovered and scrubbed every inch of the house. She remembered waking up the next morning feeling as though life couldn't possibly get any worse.

She took a minute to absorb her bedroom. In the end, she'd mustered up enough courage to take her grandmother's old room, and now that she'd teamed ocean blue and pale pink with the light-grey walls, it'd taken on a calming, tranquil feel, which Abigail loved.

Glancing into the other two bedrooms, she could visualise how they would look once they were furnished. The pale-grey carpet that was in her bedroom was also in the other two, along with the light-grey walls but, having reached her preferred budget, she was holding off buying furniture for them just yet.

Her thoughts turned to Joanna, Libby, Grace, and Georgia. It would be wonderful to have them visit, although she did wonder if there would be enough to keep the self-confessed city girls occupied at Lochside.

Tipping the coffee pot over her mug, she took a seat at the breakfast bar.

This was probably her favourite room in the entire house, or was it her writing room? She could never quite decide. But the inspiration she gained living by the loch was worth its weight in gold. The final draft of her current novel, written in only a few short months, was all the proof needed.

She admired her kitchen. Modern and sleek, but still in keeping with the house her grandmother had loved so much. Abigail was still confused about the reclusive existence her grandmother had led. She often wondered if her grandmother had realised that, by default, Abigail had been just as hidden away, just as reclusive.

Her biggest achievement by far was breaking free, escaping into the big city, and having the courage to make a life for herself in a world that was so far flung from what she'd known.

The crowds, the constant noise, and the buzz had been deafening when Abigail had first arrived in London. But that life-changing achievement had far outweighed any success she'd achieved as a writer.

Still sipping at her coffee, she wandered out to the rear garden. A work in progress, she concluded, but at least she could walk around it now without being attacked by nettles and overgrown thorny shrubs. She sat on one of her grandmother's old benches and looked back at the house, absorbing it properly for the first time now she didn't have to concentrate so much on the garden.

She let her eyes scan the rear porch. Jamie was coming around later to help her with its third and, hopefully, final coat of paint. That would then be another job ticked off her thankfully shrinking list.

But as her eyes swept across the contours of the house, they were drawn to a window – a small window, only about a foot square – sitting just above the kitchen.

That's odd, she mused. There are no windows in the attic. Of that, she was sure! And, given the number of times she'd been up there in the last few months, she should know.

But as her eyes darted across the roofline, she spotted another window. It was identical to the other, sitting just above the dining end of the kitchen. Abigail jumped to her feet and, running around the house, she found another two: one above the smallest bedroom, and another above hers.

She realised they were all situated at the rear of the house. And, given that the time she'd spent in the rear garden had been either to survey the chaos or work on the old flower borders and vegetable beds, she'd never thought to look up.

Running into the house, she sped up the hall and opened the attic hatch. Pulling on the folding ladder, she climbed up, two rungs at a time.

At first glance, there wasn't a window in sight. But as

Abigail studied the attic space, she realised that it was roughly half the size of the house.

Confused and, quite frankly, astonished she hadn't noticed this before, she clambered back down the ladder and hurried towards the back of the house, tapping on walls and checking in the back of cupboards as she went, searching for any sign of an old staircase.

But thinking back to her younger years, there had never been stairs! And her grandmother had always referred to her home as a bungalow.

Scrambling back up the ladder, Abigail began moving the few bits and pieces she'd stored in the attic away from the back wall. Wooden sheets – MDF, she presumed – created the barrier. She took her fist and knocked her way along the length of the wall. Hollow. There was the odd, solid tone, but that was only where the MDF was nailed into position, so she presumed there must be strut boards of some sort behind.

Scanning the edges, she hoped to see a gap, but the boards were flush with the walls and ceiling.

Why would her grandmother have wanted to block off part of the attic? It just didn't make any sense! And, as Abigail pondered her recent discovery, she thought it was just as odd that her grandmother had not fitted a door. Abigail was bursting with questions! But she knew the only thing to do was to take down the false wall.

The sheer number of screws holding the wall in place meant she didn't have the means to take down the wall herself, not without a trip to a DIY store.

But she did know someone who could, and he was due shortly. She sent Jamie a text. 'Hi, please can you bring your drill with you, you're never gonna believe what I've just found! Oh, and a torch.'

Chapter Twenty

By the time Jamie arrived, Abigail was sitting impatiently on the decking, quite reminiscent of how she'd spent much of her childhood.

But, instead of her grandmother's old Renault Clio churning up the dirt track, it was Jamie, in the pre-loved truck he'd recently acquired for his boating business.

He'd barely brought the vehicle to a stop when Abigail was opening his door.

'What's the rush?' He laughed.

But Abigail just threw him a cheeky grin and, grabbing his arm, pulled him towards the side of the house. 'Look!' She outstretched her arm.

Jamie's gaze followed her finger. 'What am I supposed to be looking a— Oh!'

Still gripping his arm, she led him to the back garden. 'And look, there's another, and another.' Before he could say a word, she'd dragged him around to the other side of the house and was showing him the final window. 'And if you think that's odd, just wait till you see the attic!'

Jamie followed Abigail into the attic, listening while she gushed her many theories surrounding the fake wall.

'Did you bring your drill?'

He didn't say anything.

'Jamie, Jamie, did you bring the drill? We need to open it. Now!' And with that, she was clambering back down the ladder and rushing towards the truck.

Jamie stood, cupping his face in his hands while his stomach heaved. He knew he only had a few short minutes before Abigail returned with his drill. What could he tell her? How much could he tell her? And, more importantly, would it be safe to tell her anything at all?

As he wrestled with his conscience, the advice given by hospital specialists six years ago spun in his head as though it were yesterday. He felt sick.

Trying to retake control of the situation, Jamie began to reassure himself. Maybe there was nothing to tell? Maybe there was nothing behind the wall? Maybe he was worrying over nothing?

But he knew. He knew there was no going back. He had to tell her, and he had to tell her everything. It would be far worse if they took the wall down and she was unprepared for what she might find. He'd no idea how that would affect her memories

146

but, this way, he could lessen the impact. Let her come to terms with what happened slowly.

'Here it is!' Abigail announced. 'Where should we start?'

'Abi.' There was an urgency in his voice. 'Abi, before we go taking down the wall, we need to talk.'

'Why? What's wrong?'

Not a word was spoken as he led her outside and down to the jetty. He signalled for her to sit beside him as he lowered himself down onto one of the waterproof cushions she'd bought after the old jetty was replaced, his legs dangling so his trainers sat just above the cold Atlantic Ocean.

Nervously, she lowered herself beside him. 'Jamie, you're scaring me. What is it?'

The distorted reflection from the mountains at the other side of the loch stretched across the water towards them, the autumnal golds turning to winter browns. Ducks bobbed in the swelling tide as they swam calmly beneath the jetty in stark contrast to the panic above.

Slowly, he turned to face her. 'Abi, you are my best friend. You always have been, and I love you more than you will ever know. The hardest thing I've ever had to do was let you get to know me all over again.'

Abigail felt her stomach lurch.

'It's your memories, Abi. The doctors said that we were to let you remember in your own time. That we weren't to rush you. And-and they warned us that some of your memories may never come back.'

Tears brimmed in her eyes. She was afraid, afraid of the words coming from Jamie's lips, and afraid of the world he was about to unlock. She forced herself to ask the dreaded question. 'What, what do you mean, *the doctors*?'

'Abi, I…' His gaze fell back to the water and the petite ripples left by ducks that, over the last few months, had come to feel at ease in their presence. The resident heron balanced on one leg as it stood ready to pounce on its prey.

He lingered, focussing on the darkness below as though it held within it the power to conjure up the words he struggled to find. 'They said that if your memories didn't come back, that was your body's way of protecting you, and that we should let that process happen naturally, if it was ever going to happen at all.'

Fear prevented her from asking the questions spinning ferociously, begging to be asked. Aware she was shaking, jittering almost, she pulled her jacket tighter around her as if cocooning herself from the world Jamie was about to unburden.

'I-I don't know what to say, Abi. I don't know what's behind that wall. I honestly didn't know it was there, but I'm guessing you're going to find clues – a lot of clues – to your past and to what happened here.'

Falling silent, he looked to the mountains in the distance and seemed to find the courage to continue. 'And-and there's a good chance they could bring back horrendous memories. If you want me to remove the wall, you need to be prepared for what you might find.'

He turned to face her, locking eyes and holding her gaze.

'You can't tell me not to remove it today and then go and do it yourself when I'm not here. I-I'm the only one who can tell you what happened that day.'

Abigail hung on his every word, knowing she was on the brink of facing a past that had eluded her for so long. Terrified of how her future would unfold if her memories were to come flooding back. Petrified at the thought of discovering the truth about her lost years at Lochside.

Given Jamie's demeanour, it was obvious he wasn't about to tell her everything had been rosy.

But Abigail knew there was no going back. Not now. How could she ever settle, knowing there was so much Jamie knew about her past and that the secret to unlocking that past quite possibly lay within her own four walls?

Managing to muster up a nod, Abigail gave Jamie the permission he needed to open old wounds, destabilise her existence at Lochside, and unburden what he knew.

Putting his arm around her, he pulled her close.

'Do you remember your grandfather?'

'No, he died before I was born,' she replied with conviction.

'No. No, he didn't.'

Her eyes bore into his, confused, but at the same time, pleading for him to go on. 'What? He's alive?'

'No, no he isn't, but…'

'But what?'

'He and your grandmother were separated – had been for as long as I can remember. He'd occasionally appear for a few days, if he needed to hide out, but then he'd disappear again for months at a time, sometimes years. Occasionally, your mother would come with him.'

'My mother?'

'Yeah! Abi, you-your mum was in with a bad lot. She and your grandfather would come and go as and when it suited them. But they always brought trouble with them.' His words faltered. 'They caused your grandmother a lot of stress and heartache over the years.'

He took a deep breath, as though to muster the courage to continue. 'Your grandfather used your grandmother, and this house, every time he needed to lie low for a while. He'd just appear, and your grandmother would put up with it for the sake of a quiet life. I think she always thought if this was his safe place, that he'd protect it. That he'd never bring any trouble back with him. But unfortunately, that wasn't always the case.'

'What do you mean, *lie low*? W-why would he have to lie low?'

'He was in with a bad lot, always in trouble with the police, or worse.'

'*Worse?*'

'He often owed money or favours to dangerous people and if he couldn't give them what they wanted when they came to collect, he'd come and hide out here.'

Her gaze fell to the water as her emotions flitted between anger and heartbreak. Anger at her grandfather for treating her grandmother the way he had, and heartbreak for the sheltered life her grandmother had been forced to live. 'So, what happened?'

Jamie seemed to find it easier to tell her about her past

if he looked away. He let his gaze fall across the loch and the encroaching tide. 'Your grandmother tried to keep herself to herself, but when it came to your mother, she couldn't cut the tie.'

'Why not?'

'Deep-down, she always hoped she could save her, help her turn her life around. She used to pour her heart out to my gran. At the end of the day, she was just a mother, never wanting to give up on her child.'

He pulled her closer. 'Our grandmothers were close, had been all their lives. People around here knew your grandfather was trouble, Abi, but I promise you, no one other than our grandparents, my parents – and me – knew just how much trouble he was. And-and no one other than us, and the police, know what happened that day.'

'The police. Wh-what day?'

'Your grandmother led a quiet life. She didn't want to draw attention to herself, or you. She didn't want to make herself easy to find if any of your grandfather's unsavoury contacts decided to wreak revenge. She had to protect you, keep you safe. You were even home-schooled here – she was that scared of something happening to you. That's why she kept you here. That's why you've no memories of going to school or anywhere else. And she succeeded too, until you were about eleven. That's when your grandfather first found her and started using the house the way he did.'

'But what day? What day are you talking about?'

Jamie shuffled around to face her properly and let out

a long sigh. 'You were twenty-three. Your grandmother was washing dishes, and you were getting ready. We, erm, you and I, were supposed to be going for a hike.'

'But-but you told me that we knew each other from when we were young, until about eleven?'

'I know, I'm sorry. I-I panicked. I didn't know what to say.'

She detected a change in his tone as he took her hand tightly in his. 'I didn't want to risk jolting your memory, Abi. I didn't know what you knew at that point and, after what the doctors had said, I-I couldn't just ask. And it was obvious that first day, when I brought you the groceries, that you didn't recognise me.'

Abigail could see the anguish in Jamie as he unburdened her past. He was pale and seemed to be more panicked about what was still to be said than what he'd already told her. 'There's worse to come, isn't there?'

'Look, Abi.'

'You never call me Abi?'

'I *always* called you Abi!' he retorted, rather more harshly than intended.

He was usually able to keep his emotions in check, but tears welled in his eyes. As an ex-soldier, he was always together, in control of his emotions. But, today, he struggled to compose himself.

'That day, I was supposed to be here for eight thirty. We were going to cross the loch, by boat, and then hike up to that ridge.' He nodded towards one of the smaller hills in the distance.

'But, I'—he hung his head—'I was running late. Someone had slashed my tyres. I texted you and said I'd be closer to ten and...'

'And what?'

Jamie's eyes bore into the water, but he saw nothing other than the scene that had met him that day.

'And what?' Abigail demanded.

'And-and when I got here...'

'Please, Jamie.'

'The front door was broken. It'd been pushed in. I ran through the house looking for you and—' He stopped and, if it were at all possible, tightened his grip on her yet again, as though it would in some way protect her from his words. 'I found you lying in the hall, and your grandmother lying in the kitchen, just beside the kitchen door.

'You were both unconscious, and the house had been ransacked. I have no idea what happened that day other than what your grandmother was able to tell the police once she regained consciousness.'

'Wh-what did she say?'

But he hadn't heard her. He was lost in his thoughts and the trauma of that day. 'I called for an ambulance and the police. They were just arriving when your grandmother came around, but I couldn't wake you, Abi. Nothing I did brought you back.

'I went with you in the ambulance while the police got to work checking the house for any clues as to what happened, or who did it. They dusted the place for fingerprints, but there were only yours, mine, and your grandparents.'

'My dad came here so there was someone overseeing what was

happening and, once the police were finished, he called in a favour and had the door replaced and the house secured that same day.'

Jamie closed his eyes tightly, trying to come to terms with the fact he was doing exactly what the doctors had warned him against, and loathing himself for it.

He loved Abigail – she was the most important person in the world to him – and he was tearing her world apart. 'If-if only I'd been on time, Abi. Maybe I could've done something. Maybe your grandmother would still be here today.'

'Or maybe you'd be dead.' Her words were a whisper. It was all she could manage as she searched her past for a glimmer of a memory that reflected Jamie's words. Still nothing.

'They discharged your grandmother the next day, but she sat by your bed for-for weeks, Abi.'

'Weeks!' She felt sick and weak, but she needed him to continue. She needed to hear all that he had to say. She still didn't fully understand the link between this and her grandmother's death.

He nodded. 'You'd received quite a blow to your head and, going by other bruising on your body, the doctors reckoned you'd put up quite a fight.'

Sitting in silence, she let Jamie's words sink in, allowing herself to comprehend the full horror of what had gone on at Lochside. 'Who did it?'

'They never found them, but the police reckoned there were two vehicles, going by the tracks left outside, and they came for two things.'

'But-but what on earth would my grandmother have that someone would be prepared to go to these lengths for?'

'It wasn't your grandmother they were after, Abi. Your grandfather had turned up the day before and the police reckon he'd been followed. He was found the same day I found you.'

Abigail interrupted. 'What do you mean, *found*?'

'His body was found in the woods about half a mile from the house. He'd been shot in the back. The police reckoned whoever did it probably wanted him dead, especially given he'd made a run for it and left you and your grandmother alone in the house. But, as the house was also ransacked, they thought that whoever did it was also looking for something, which would make sense, given your grandfather's track record.'

Abigail sat in silence as she fought to process Jamie's words. Fought to grasp the fact that her grandfather had led such an unsavoury existence.

'I was twenty-three?'

Jamie nodded.

'But I don't remember my teenage years here at all. Maybe up to about eleven or twelve, but that's it.'

Jamie took a long, slow, deep breath. How much more should he tell her? How much of her past life would she find behind the attic wall? How deep into her teenage years should he take her?

'When you finally came round, your memory had been affected. *Dissociative amnesia*, the doctors called it. You appeared to have blotted out the years where your grandfather had come

155

and gone, which meant you remembered nothing from the age of around eleven onwards. You—'

She watched intently as he struggled to finish his sentence.

'You didn't remember us, Abi. We were wiped out, along with the missing years.'

As Abigail absorbed his words, she knew he was telling the truth. And while she finally had an explanation for her lack of memories and for a past that had escaped her, she was filled with rage for a stranger who had only been her grandfather by name.

She wanted to scream. She wanted to shout. But there was no one to hear, no one who deserved it, anyway.

They sat in silence. An eternity seemed to pass them by before Abigail finally spoke again. 'What happened next?'

'Sometime after you regained consciousness, you were to be allowed home, but only because your grandmother was there to look after you. As you were being wheeled out to the ambulance to come home, she had a massive heart attack. It happened at the hospital and doctors were there within minutes, but there was nothing they could do.'

Jamie's gaze searched the loch, the hills in the distance, and the shoreline that led to the open sea. He was doing all he could to avoid her gaze. 'It meant they had to keep you in for longer, and by the time you were ready to be discharged, you didn't want to come back here. You barely remembered it. So,'—he paused—'you went to the reading of your grandmother's will and, after your mother came and claimed all the furniture, you got in your car and left. I never saw you after that. Not until you came back a few months ago.'

'How do you know all this? I mean, I don't remember seeing you? You must have stayed away?'

'I hung around the hospital unless they shooed me off. But, yeah, I did. Reluctantly. On doctor's orders, I kept my distance. But this is Skye, Abi. People talk.'

Abigail sat, absorbing his words, crying for the life her grandmother had led and the years she'd lost to a blow to the head. She fell limp into Jamie's hold and in return, he leaned his head on hers, still holding her tightly.

He wondered whether he should go deeper. Would it make any difference to how she felt? Would it help her to make sense of how things were back then? And would she find out anyway when they took away the wall?

Deciding he had no option, Jamie continued. 'I sat by your bedside every day, Abi, while they let me. Hoping that one day you would waken up and remember. Remember me. Remember us, but you never did.'

Jamie knew Abigail could remember nothing other than her grandmother's heart attack, and she could remember that as clear as day.'

'Did-did they find what they were looking for?'

'What?'

'The people who did it. Did they find what they were looking for?'

The pain Jamie had felt at losing Abigail had been all-consuming and, just as it was resurfacing once again, he realised his words hadn't registered quite the way he'd intended. 'We don't know. The police couldn't find anything belonging to your grandad other than a rucksack. There were only a few pieces of clothing in it, so they presumed he either wasn't intending on staying long or he'd had to get away quickly and hadn't had time to pack anything else. But the police felt at the time there might have been something else in the rucksack and the intruders had already found it. I mean, why ransack the place if you're not looking for anything?'

Ignoring the darkening clouds, the stirring water, and the cooling North Atlantic winds, Jamie kept his arm around her, comforting her from both the elements that were now sweeping down from the open sea, and a past she couldn't connect with.

Minutes felt like hours. And Jamie kept hoping Abigail would ask the question. If she didn't, should he volunteer the information, anyway? Maybe her not knowing was for the best, but then again, what clues to her past lay hidden behind the false wall? Was it not better that she heard it from him?

'Thank you.'

'For what?'

'For being there. For getting help. For staying with me all those weeks while I was unconscious, and for hanging around the hospital after I woke up, even when I didn't know who you were.'

'There-there's something else, Abi.'

*

Abigail lifted her head, surveying his expression and wondering what on earth he could have left to add to the horrendous events that had stolen so many years from her. But his expression had changed; he'd become vulnerable.

'What-what is it?'

'Abi—'

'Please, tell me.' She encouraged him softly.

'Look, I don't know what's behind that wall. Maybe there's nothing. But, then again, maybe there's something. And, if that's the case, then it's far better you hear it from me.' He took a deep breath, as though to dislodge the words. 'We were engaged!'

'Engaged.'

Jamie seemed to be trying desperately to hold her gaze. Was he desperate for a flicker of recognition?

Abigail eased herself from his comforting grasp. Jamie's words were spinning in her head, churning up fear, heartache, and a new understanding of the existence both she and her grandmother had endured at Lochside. And now this. Nothing was as it had seemed!

As she looked into his pleading eyes, she could only think of how he'd watched as she'd tried to make a home. How he'd watched as she'd tried to start over in a place that'd caused her so much pain. And, more importantly, how he'd stayed quiet in a world that she'd been trying so desperately to understand.

He'd watched as she'd fought to come to terms with where she'd come from, and who she was, and he hadn't said a word. He hadn't been honest with her.

Chapter Twenty-One

Abigail was now out of time. The fifth dress she'd tried on was going to have to stay on as Greg's car came to a halt outside. A few minutes later, she heard his familiar rattle on the door.

Trying desperately to shake her vexed mood, Abigail forced a smile and opened the door. Greg seemed to sense, though, that her mood hadn't improved since their walk the previous afternoon.

'Hey, how are you?' he asked cautiously.

'Fine!'

'You sure?'

'I said *I'm fine*, didn't I!'

'Look, we don't have to go out if you don't want to. We could order in, instead?'

A pang of guilt ripped through her as she hurried into

the bedroom to grab her bag. This wasn't her! This wasn't how she usually treated people and, if she were honest, it was only making her feel worse. 'Sorry,' she whispered, more from exasperation and exhaustion than anything else. She'd barely slept since Jamie had left a couple of days ago, just after she'd run inside and locked the door on him.

'Look, if something's wrong, you can tell me. You can trust me, I promise.' He put his arm around her waist and pulled her close.

'It's okay. I'm fine, honestly.' She tried to reassure him. 'I just haven't been sleeping that well, that's all. Let's go.'

But as she turned the key in the lock, she couldn't help but picture someone breaking down the door. Blotting the image from her mind, she turned her attention towards Greg's car. As usual, he'd opened her door and was waiting for her to take her seat.

'Thank you, but you don't have to do that, you know.'

'I know.' He smiled as if trying to carry on like nothing was wrong. 'How do you fancy Indian for dinner? Then that movie you mentioned is on later, if you feel like it?'

A movie might be a welcome distraction, she concluded. They wouldn't have to fill the entire night with small talk. 'Yes, that would be nice.'

Greg pulled out onto the main road before reaching across and taking her hand in his. 'I know something's wrong, Abigail. If you don't want to talk about it, fine, but at least tell me if I've done something wrong.'

Abigail was aware she was rolling her eyes. He could be so

needy sometimes. 'Look, there's nothing for you to worry about. It's just book stuff, that's all. And I'd rather not talk about it. It'll sort itself out, one way or the other.'

The miles rolled by much quieter than usual, and it felt as though an age had passed before Greg finally pulled in just a few short metres away from the restaurant.

Greg was only level with the bonnet when she opened her door and let herself out. She had no time for that nonsense, she decided, and this was the night that she was going to put a stop to it, once and for all.

The cold November evening made her shiver in the few short steps it took for them to walk from the car to the restaurant. And she knew Greg was being cautious as he held the door open for her before following Mr Yadavalli to their table. She was sure he was thinking that tonight wasn't exactly going to be plain sailing.

The secluded corner was every inch the romantic setting, and Abigail knew that if she were in a better mood, she would have probably succumbed to the atmosphere, and the tone for the evening would have been set.

Mr Yadavalli gave them a few minutes before returning to take their drink orders.

'Just a Coke, please.'

'You don't fancy anything else, a wine or—'

'A Coke please', she reiterated looking only at Mr Yadavalli.

'I'll have the same.'

Mr Yadavalli nodded before leaving them to peruse their menus. Greg seemed grateful for the distraction, turning his

162

attention to the main courses.

Abigail finally broke the silence. 'Have you always lived here? In town, I mean.'

'No. I-I came here about-about six years ago.'

Abigail noticed how reluctantly he seemed to divulge the information. 'Why, what brought you here?'

He shrugged. 'I just fancied a fresh start, that's all.'

'Why here?'

'Why not?'

'Did you know anyone before you came?'

'No, no. Why?' he said, his expression serious.

'Just wondering. What did you do when you first arrived?'

'I found work and a place to stay. You know the drill. You decided what you want to eat yet?'

'Where did you work? Did you not bring your business with you?'

'No.' He looked uncomfortable.

'Oh, so where did you work, before you started your tiling business?'

'I, eh, I got a job with a guy called Mike Scanlan.'

'Who's he?'

'Just my old boss. I took over after he died.' His responses now seemed robotic, rehearsed almost.

'Died?'

'Yeah, he fell from a ladder. Died instantly.'

'Oh, that's awful!'

'Yeah, it was. I ended up taking over his client list and staying. The end!' He smirked.

Mr Yadavalli, appearing to silently float into Abigail's peripheral vision, caused her to jump, while at the same time, bringing an end to their conversation.

After ordering their choice of main courses — a chicken biryani for Greg and a chicken pasanda for Abigail, with a side order of mixed pakora to share – Greg seemed to be trying to keep the conversation light. Abigail sipped at her Coke and commented on their surroundings.

Deciding to force Jamie's recent revelations to the back of her mind, she made every effort to enjoy her evening and the welcome distraction it offered.

The warm red décor and dark wood furnishings gave the spacious room an intimate feel. Oversized decorative planters with equally oversized areca and parlour palms gave a sense of privacy and seclusion to the tables, which enabled Abigail to switch off a little.

'I need to buy a car!' she blurted out.

'A car, oh okay. What were you thinking?'

'Just something small and economical. I just wasn't sure where to go around here.'

'Well, there's a couple of garages on the mainland. I could go with you if you want?'

'That would be good. Are you free over the next day or two?'

'Eh, yeah, I've got a couple of jobs on, but I could move them around a bit. Could we go early morning?'

'Yeah, the time doesn't matter to me, just whenever suits.' She shrugged.

'Okay, pick you up at nine tomorrow then.'

Abigail nodded. 'Great, thanks.'

'What's brought this on?' Greg enquired.

'Oh, nothing really. I just thought it was about time I was a little less reliant on others to get around, that's all.'

The rest of the evening passed rather better than it'd started. Getting out of the house had been just the distraction Abigail had needed, and by the time they were leaving the cinema, she'd returned to her normal cheery self.

Greg wrapped his arm around her waist as they strolled back to his car. It was reassuring. She felt safe. He tightened his grip, his hand now clasping her ribs. She leaned into him, allowing her head to rest on his chest as they continued in silence, tingling with lustful excitement as she inhaled his scent.

Wrapping her arm around his front, she drew him closer, as if never wanting to let him go. A wave of desire swept across her, a desire to be held, to be touched, to be loved, to be lost in another world, even if only for a short while.

As they reached the car, Greg clicked to unlock it but seemed to have decided against holding her door open. Instead, he caressed the small of her back tenderly before they made their way to their own sides of the car.

There wasn't the usual chatter as Greg drove them back to Lochside. The darkness and the quiet road only added to their silence. Abigail could feel the sexual tension in the air. It was tantalising, teasing. She couldn't wait to get home.

As Greg guided the car out of the town and onto the quieter roads, he reached across. Instinctively, she opened her hand to take his, but his fell gently to her knee instead. Her wrap dress allowed his fingertips to caress her skin. She gasped. Embarrassed, she tried to control her breathing, but it was too late. He'd heard her response and, in turn, he responded by gently gliding his hand further up her leg. Stroking it gently.

Her body tingled, her leg fell limply towards him, and his fingers travelled deeper, caressing her inner thigh. She groaned, biting her lower lip. Every inch of her shivered with excitement. She longed for him to kiss her, to take her. She longed for their journey to be over.

Greg had barely come to a halt at Lochside when he reached across. Their lips became entwined in a kiss that left neither of them in any doubt as to what the other wanted.

Chapter Twenty-Two

The warmth from the coffee mug cupped between Abigail's hands did little to stave off the early morning chill or the deep-seated feeling of regret that was currently wallowing in the pit of her stomach.

As the loch sprang to life, Abigail fell into her grandmother's old wicker chair, which had once again taken up residence at the far end of the jetty.

She pulled a blanket over her cooling body. Never in all the time since she'd returned to Lochside had she woken so early. She sipped slowly at her coffee, savouring every mouthful, as she watched the ducks emerge from their slumber.

She couldn't help but chuckle as they dipped their heads below water before shaking the excess off after they re-emerged, face washed and ready for their day. If only it were that simple.

She sighed.

She'd spent most of the night tossing and turning and dreading nine o'clock when Greg would return to pick her up. He'd been completely oblivious to her vivid realisation, and to how close she'd come to blurting out the wrong name.

After walking her to the decking, the sexual chemistry that'd been so provocatively arousing during their silent journey home had only intensified. Greg's lips had travelled from the corners of Abigail's mouth to her earlobes and down her neck, before finding their way back to her warm eager mouth.

His hands had caressed her hips, her buttocks, and her thighs, before they'd travelled upwards again, grasping her ribcage, and teasing the outer edges of her breasts.

She'd gasped when his thumbs had glided ever closer to her nipples and had felt herself go limp when he'd given in to his desire to touch them. He'd stroked them, fondled them, had enjoyed their hardness as he teased them through her dress and skimpy lace bra.

He'd reacted to her gasps. He'd ground into her. And she'd groaned as he'd pushed her gently towards the door. It'd fallen open and together they'd rushed to her bedroom.

She could remember the desire she'd felt as he untied the front of her dress and removed her bra while she unzipped and removed his jeans.

She'd been aware of his hardness; it had reacted to its release. And she could remember them throwing their clothes to the floor and her absorbing every inch of his torso.

His lips had travelled downwards from hers. They'd moved

fleetingly over her chin, down her neck, and onto her cleavage where they'd lingered, his tongue teasing as it'd lusted over her breasts.

His warm breath had continued down her body. His lips, kissing her warm, pale skin, had made their way down her slender toned torso. She'd shivered in anticipation as they'd flitted over her belly button and nestled themselves just above her hairline. They'd teased, making her jerk with excitement, before his tongue and lips had combined to travel seductively back to her nipples.

He'd sat back on his knees, admiring her, stroking her. And she'd taken him in her hands as it'd become his turn to groan. His turn to lose himself in her grasp as she caressed him until he fell by her side.

And, just as his groans had been about to give way to exhilaration, she'd mounted him. Her damp breasts had glistened above him in the moonlight, and she knew he had almost given in to the moment.

But, instead, he'd stopped her, had brought her lips to his and had rolled her over. Her back had arched instinctively as she felt his hot breath tingling on her damp skin. His tongue had travelled up her breast and circled her nipple before he'd taken its hardness in his mouth. At the same time, his hand had travelled downwards towards her hairline and the dampness that lay beneath. His fingers invading. His mouth still lavishing her breast.

She remembered shivering as he'd brought his lips back to hers before her legs had fallen open, allowing him inside her. She

169

remembered how she'd shuddered with exhilaration when they had come together.

It had been the most erotic and sexual experience of her life and it had been with the wrong man.

Chapter Twenty-Three

Almost two weeks had passed since Abigail and Greg had taken their relationship to the next level. And, as with every other morning since, Abigail was wondering what on earth she'd done.

Stepping from the shower, she wrapped herself in a towel and bundled her hair into a clip. She realised she had to face her feelings once and for all, and, as she set about getting dressed, she tried desperately to work out exactly what these feelings might be.

Greg was a great guy. He was handsome, kind, thoughtful, attentive – a bit too attentive at times, which she often found irritating. But as she pondered her feelings, she couldn't deny she cared for him. They got along most of the time, and he did appear to be realising that she liked her independence. But was it love? After all, it wasn't his name she'd almost blurted out!

And speaking of love, there was Jamie. He hadn't been in touch since that day on the jetty, and Abigail couldn't help but wonder if she'd lost him for good.

He'd been the reliable constant in her life since she'd returned to Lochside, and to say she was missing him was an understatement. But, whenever she'd attempted to interpret her past or had struggled with her memories, he'd chosen to stay silent.

As she grabbed a pair of jeans and a pastel pink hoodie, she wondered if she'd perhaps overreacted. She could hear his words: *The doctors said we were to let you remember in your own time. That we weren't to rush you.*

She repeated his words as she applied her moisturiser and blow-dried her hair. And reflected on the days since she'd discovered the truth about her missing years.

There had been no sudden flood of memories; not even a flicker, which she had to admit, she was finding frustrating.

And, perhaps more surprisingly, her desperation to find out what was behind the hidden wall had also disappeared. She wasn't sure if she would ever want to know. It now felt as though she would be opening old wounds, releasing memories her grandmother had wanted keeping secret.

Greg had also been around a lot more. He'd taken their night of passion to indicate a far more significant shift in their relationship than Abigail had. And if she were to be completely honest with herself, she couldn't help but wonder if, after all Jamie had told her on the jetty, that she hadn't just needed to feel loved.

Greg had gone with Abigail to look at cars and had helped her decide on a lightning-blue Ford Fiesta. It was only three years old, had low mileage, and was in great condition thanks to its one elderly owner. And Greg had been great at reassuring her when she'd been nervous about driving it home.

She'd sold her car when she'd arrived in London, to help with her deposit when she'd moved in with Georgia. And once she met Darren, he'd done most of the driving. When she'd needed to go anywhere on her own, it'd always been much easier to hop on a bus. That was just London life. Most people hopped on a bus or took the Tube.

But as the days had passed, her confidence had begun to return. She'd initially found it unnerving. She couldn't remember her driving lessons or taking her test but, as with so many things, the skills learned were embedded in her subconscious. If she didn't overthink it, she could do it. She was, however, enjoying the freedom of going wherever she wanted, whenever she wanted.

Scolding herself, she tried to get her thoughts back on track. Being mobile didn't exactly help her quandary any. And, as she studied her reflection and added the final touches to her make-up, she was hit by a sudden realisation. Would she feel the same if it'd been Greg who'd betrayed her in that way? And, more importantly, would she be this upset if it'd been Greg who'd disappeared from her life? Actually, did she even want Greg in her life?

As she asked herself these questions, she realised that *betrayed* was perhaps too strong a word. For the first time, she began to wonder if she would have acted any differently if the shoe had been on the other foot.

She contemplated the thought while she added a pair of small, silver stud earrings and a bracelet to her outfit. No matter how she felt, Jamie had been acting on doctor's advice. And who was she to argue with a medical professional?

Retreating to her writing room, she thought about her plan for the day: writing until three and then a quick trip into Portree for some shopping.

Switching on her laptop, she sorted through her notes from the previous day's writing as she waited for it to come to life. She was editing, filling in the gaps in her manuscript, and making sure she had no loose ends. It was a process she enjoyed, unlike some other authors she knew.

Re-reading her notes, she realised she was reading the same line over and over, her thoughts insisting on returning to Jamie. Was she in love with him? Or was she just missing his friendship?

Elbows on her desk, she held her head in her hands. She wasn't the kind of person to string someone along, and she did like Greg. Possibly, if Jamie had never been on the scene, Greg would've been the one. After all, he did tick a lot of the right boxes when it came to what she would hope to find in a man. But there was just no—just no…She repeated the words over and over in her head until her sentence was involuntarily completed. There was just no spark!

Leaning back in her chair, she gazed out over the loch. It

reminded her of Jamie, of their friendship, and the unnerving probability she was in love with him.

Could she make a life here at Lochside knowing that the man she wanted was just a few miles along the coast? And what if they never made up? What if their friendship had been damaged beyond repair? Abigail felt an ache in the pit of her stomach; the thought of Jamie not being in her life was unbearable.

Then there was Greg. How could she stay with Greg, knowing he was her second choice? That wasn't fair to him.

As if playing ping-pong, her thoughts darted off in the opposite direction. Should she just stay quiet? Should she stay with Greg, knowing he adored her? Knowing they got on well together, but knowing he was never the one?

Abigail rose from her chair. Her precious jetty calling her, she grabbed a jacket. She'd been writing long enough to know that when she couldn't fully concentrate, the best thing to do was walk away.

Staring into the dark, broken reflection of the choppy waters, she hoped upon hope that she could make everything right. She knew staying at Lochside would be unbearable if Jamie wasn't in her life. And at that point, she knew, if she couldn't repair her friendship with him, she'd have to go back to the city.

But a nauseous panic stirring in the pit of her stomach reminded her she'd started over once before.

Chapter Twenty-Four

To say the city lights had been a culture shock for Abigail would have been putting it mildly.

She'd arrived late afternoon to find gridlock and tempers flailing as horns tooted and traffic and pedestrians intermingled in a cacophony of chaos.

After driving down the M6 past Manchester and Birmingham and the multitude of lanes she'd had to contend with, she'd naively thought that arriving in London would be a relief.

But driving in past Luton and Watford, towards Camden, had left her a shattered wreck. And so, after finding a place to park and a café, Abigail stopped for a much-needed rest.

A bowl of tepid soup and a sandwich had done little to satisfy her as panic surged at the thought of finding a decent place to stay in the metropolis.

Had she ever been to London? She had no idea. Did she know anyone in London? No idea. A future landlord would want information, but what information? And could she provide it?

Abigail had fumbled through letting sites on her phone, but her lack of memories had meant she found even the simplest of tasks daunting.

The waitress had come to clear the table. 'We close at five. Just letting you know,' the pleasant voice attached to the eclectic outfit and long, untamed hair had told her.

She'd had no idea she'd been in the café for so long. It was all becoming too much, again. She'd felt so small, sitting in a strange café, in a small corner of a vast city, nestled in a country, floating in an ocean that led to a world where she remembered no one. Not a living soul!

She could remember paying, but the rest of the evening had been a blur. She'd phoned around hostels, bed and breakfasts, small hotels, but all were fully booked. Before she knew it, her mobile was out of battery.

And having spent the night in her car, she found herself back in the same café the following morning. The same bohemian outfit served her breakfast. 'Gosh, you don't look so good,' the pleasant voice had commented. 'Are you feeling okay?'

Abigail still couldn't quite remember the order of events. She knew she'd only just left the hospital and had lost her grandmother; could recall a woman – an older version of the mother from her childhood – clearing the house and her journey to London. But what else? She was still getting headaches.

Other than recalling memories of when she was a young child, it was as though she'd never existed. Whenever a decision had to be made, panic would envelop her in a whirlwind of nausea, sweats, palpitations, and breathlessness.

The bohemian waitress asking her if she was okay had resulted in those very symptoms. Abigail had been plied with water to sip and was told she could sit as long as she liked while the bohemian waitress made a few calls.

Sometime later, the waitress had returned, saying her sister was going to be looking for a flatmate. If she didn't mind a few nights on the sofa while the current roommate moved out, then she was welcome to look at the room.

To this day, Abigail believes that the relief she felt, and the kindness shown by Melissa, in a world she was struggling to comprehend, truly saved her. Life had been becoming unbearable and if it wasn't for the laid back bohemian waitress and her even more laid back sister, Georgia, Abigail wasn't sure she would be here today.

Chapter Twenty-Five

Autumn had well and truly set in and, if Abigail's thoughts weren't quite so focussed on mustering up the courage needed to turn left, she would probably have taken a moment to enjoy the leaves raining down on her windscreen in a multitude of golds, coppers, oranges, and yellows. It's a scene she would've normally banked, ready to transport to the pages of a manuscript.

Instead, she gripped the wheel with dogged determination and pressed lightly on the accelerator. And, when the traffic allowed, she proceeded to turn left into whatever drama was about to unfold.

All too quickly, she arrived in the village and came to a stop just outside Jamie's parents' store. Looking through the window, Abigail could see Morag standing behind the counter with the young mum Jamie had told her about, the one who worked a few hours during the week while her children were in school.

Abigail's chest pounded as she approached the door. She reminded herself she was a grown woman and could do this. She needed to pull herself together.

She felt her face flush red at Morag's look of surprise when she turned to see her nearing the counter. How much had Jamie told her? Was she no longer welcome?

'Morning, Abi. How are you?' Morag enquired, a little too cautiously for Abigail's liking.

Abigail became flustered, blushing a darker shade of red as thoughts ran through her mind: Oh god, what does she know? What must she think of me? 'I'm fine, thank you, Morag, and you?' she managed.

Morag replied with a smile and a head tilt as Abigail paused to pluck up the courage to speak again. 'I was wondering if Jamie was around?'

'He's at the boatyard.'

Smiling, Abigail remembered their barbecue on the jetty. It was one of her favourite memories and she wasn't quite sure how Jamie would feel about her rocking up unannounced as though nothing had happened. 'Ah, okay. Thanks anyway.'

Abigail turned to leave but glanced back. 'Would you mind letting him know I called by?'

'Why don't you go along to the yard? Tell him yourself?'

Abigail wasn't sure how to respond. She shrugged and shook her head. 'It's okay, I don't want to disturb him if he's working.'

'For goodness' sake. You've come this far. What's another mile?' Morag retorted, rather like a mother scolding a child. 'Go see him.'

Abigail took a deep breath. 'I'll think about it.' And with that, she was back in her car, staring into the distance and wondering if Morag was right.

In the end, Abigail concluded she was. After all, she'd come this far. And she'd been prepared to face whatever reaction she'd received in the shop, so why should the boatyard be any different?

After checking the road was clear, Abigail pulled out and continued through the village towards the boatyard. Having spent the past three weeks thinking of nothing other than her falling out with Jamie, she still had no clue as to what she would say to him.

Slowing down as she approached the yard, she scanned the sheds and jetty carefully before looking for somewhere to park. The thought of a showdown in front of anyone else was mortifying.

Biting on her lower lip as though it would quash the butterflies which were currently intermingled with a churning in the pit of her stomach, Abigail began to wonder if she was doing the right thing. Accosting him at work was perhaps not the kindest thing to do. And what if he didn't want to see her? What if he'd decided he was better off without her?

Knowing Jamie wouldn't recognise her car, she wondered if she should turn around, return to Lochside. He would be none the wiser.

But, deep-down, she knew her apprehension wasn't about the reaction she might get from Jamie. It was because she knew he could never give her the reaction she craved. He could never hold her tightly in his arms. He could never tell her he would never let her go. He was Claire's. She had to remember that. She could only appeal for his friendship, nothing else.

Stepping from her car, she spotted him coming out of one of the sheds. He hadn't noticed her; his head was down. There was still time to change her mind, still time to turn back, still time to avoid any confrontation.

'Abi?'

Too late! He was walking towards her, rubbing his hands on an old rag, and looking quite irresistible with his torn shirt, oily hands, and dishevelled hair.

He looked just as nervous and emotional as Abigail, which instantly put her at ease.

'What are you doing here?'

'I can go, if you'd rather.'

'No, please. Please stay. We need to talk.'

'I know,' she agreed. 'I just wasn't sure you'd want to.'

'You know me better than that.'

She smiled cautiously.

'You-you'd a lot to process that day, Abi. And, anyway, when you put it in the context you did, you were right. Under the circumstances, I probably should have told you sooner.' He nodded towards the jetty. 'You want to come sit for a while?'

She followed, taking in the views as she went. This part of the loch was just as alive with ducks as it was at Lochside and the views looking down from the head of the sea loch were simply stunning.

The far side was more mountainous, more rugged, and would lead you into the Cuillin's depths if you were to keep walking. The other side, her side, was a little flatter. The hills tended to roll away from the trees behind Lochside a little less dramatically than that of the mountains. But that just allowed for a different kind of beauty, and it meant she had the best of the views.

Jamie signalled towards an old bench nestled just to the jetty's left. 'I found it in one of the sheds. Needs a second lick of paint, but I'll get round to that at some point.'

Abigail took a seat beside him, aware he was just staring straight ahead. Presumably, he was just as wary as she was about where their conversation was going to lead.

'How have you been?' he eventually asked, breaking the silence.

'Fine.'

He let out a heavy sigh. Abigail was trying to decipher what it'd meant when he shifted his whole body around to face her. 'I'm sorry, Abi. I know you've not been fine. How could you be after everything I told you?'

'I'm okay, really, I am.'

But she suspected he knew her far too well and wasn't at all convinced.

'I just have so many questions.'

'Well, fire away. I'll answer what I can.'

She took a deep breath. 'First of all, I need to know about you.'

'Me?'

'You said we were engaged?'

'We were.' His gaze fell to his lap.

'It couldn't have been easy for you, when I just up and left, I mean.'

A long-drawn-out sigh escaped as his oily hands slid across his forehead. 'It wasn't. It was devastating. We-we were in love with each other. We spent every spare minute we had together. We'd only been engaged a few months, but we'd already started planning our wedding. We'd bought the cottage.'

'Cottage?'

'Yeah, we'd just had an offer accepted on a cottage.'

Abigail didn't realise he still owned it, still lived in it, and hadn't yet had the heart to sell it. Her eyes welled up, and she tried desperately to stop her tears from flowing. She wanted to hear all Jamie had to say without him thinking he had to hold back. 'And…?' She encouraged him to go on.

'And, then after that day…' He paused. 'You haven't remembered anything more since I last spoke to you?'

She shook her head.

He smiled sympathetically. 'When you left, I couldn't stay, Abi. I couldn't stay here and be reminded every day of what I'd lost, so that's when I decided to join the army.'

'Had you always wanted to be a soldier?'

'Eh, no!' He smirked. 'Never! But I needed to get away. I needed the discipline. I needed something that would consume every waking minute of my life so I wouldn't have time to think.'

There were a few moments of silence while Jamie seemed to search for the right words.

'I'm so sorry. It's breaking my heart that I can't remember us.'

'It is?'

'Yes! It is! And I'm so sorry I put you through it all.'

'It was hardly your fault. You had enough to be dealing with. It was just…I had no idea where you'd gone. No idea if you were okay. No idea if you'd managed to get a roof over your head. And-and I'd no idea if everything was okay, medically. I worried you were suffering from flashbacks or trauma or, I don't know, whatever else could happen after everything you'd been through, and that you might be dealing with it all alone.'

Abigail leaned into him. 'I'm so sorry, but I was okay. Other than I'd no memories.' She shrugged. 'I mean, there was just over a decade that I couldn't account for and-and I'd no idea why. Even though the hospital is sketchy, I remember being discharged and staying at Lochside for a couple of days. That was unbearable without my grandmother there. And scary,' she emphasised, 'given the last thing I could remember was me cycling around there as a young child.'

Jamie put his arm around her, consoling without words, allowing her to speak, to let it all out.

'I can remember not recognising my reflection in the mirror. Apart from losing my grandmother, that was probably the hardest thing. I was a stranger to myself. The clothes in my wardrobe, the trinkets in my room, had no meaning. My lack of memories protected me from everything else. It was a really weird feeling. It's not like I still thought I was a child. I knew I wasn't. I felt like an adult, but I just didn't know who that adult was.'

She took a deep breath, allowing the sea air to fill her lungs, before releasing it slowly. 'I can remember the reading of the will too,' she said emphatically. 'My mother made sure of that with all her drama and tantrums. But other than that, my memories start properly again from the moment I got in my car and left Lochside. I-I didn't set out to go to London. I just couldn't stop driving.'

Abigail noticed Jamie surveying the far side of the loch and the hills beyond, and she wondered whether they used to climb them together.

'Have you looked behind the wall yet?' he said, interrupting her thoughts.

'No.'

'Really? I thought by now your curiosity would have the better of you.'

'I know.' She smiled. 'I'd have thought the same, but I haven't been able to bring myself to go up there since, never mind take the wall down.'

'What's Greg's thoughts on it all?'

'I haven't told him.'

'You haven't told him?' Jamie's eyes widened.

'No.'

'Why? I mean, I'm just shocked, that's all.'

'I'm not sure.' She shrugged. 'How's Claire?'

'We, eh, we're on a break,' Jamie replied cautiously. 'Or, to be more accurate, I keep trying to end things with her. But she seems hell-bent on us getting back together.'

'And you? How do you feel about it?'

'Nah, she isn't for me. Never was, and I don't think I'm right for her either, to be fair.'

'I'm sorry, Jamie.' She wasn't completely lying. 'Are you okay?'

'Yeah, yeah. It was never going to last. We were too different. And, looking back, I'm ashamed to say, she was probably no more than a much-needed distraction'—he glanced fleetingly towards her—'and, deep-down, I always knew she was never that fussed about being with me, either. I should have ended it long ago. But that's why I find it strange that she wants us to get back together. Maybe she just doesn't like being on her own.'

'You think?'

'Yeah, maybe. She can be a bit hot and cold.'

Abigail pondered his words. Was that all Greg was to her? A distraction? She hadn't thought about it from that point of view. But now, as she contemplated Jamie's words, she could feel herself relating to them. 'I'm sorry, Jamie.'

'Would you stop apologising! None of this is of your making.'

Giving him an appreciative smile, she looked down the loch towards the open ocean. 'I think this is my second favourite view of the loch.'

'Only second, huh?'

To her relief, they shared a laugh that let Abigail know all was well between them.

'Why haven't you told Greg?'

Shrugging, she said, 'I don't know. I-I'm just not sure.'

'Not sure about telling him, or not sure about him?'

Wow, she thought. Straight to the point! 'Both, I guess.'

Chapter Twenty-Six

'Are you sure you're ready?' Jamie asked, drill poised.

Abigail nodded. 'Yes! Let's do this.'

Jamie studied the solid sheets of MDF and opted to start at the farthest right side. He began removing the screws that ran along the bottom, before working his way up either side.

Abigail stepped forward to catch the sheet as he began loosening the screws along the top, but the MDF stayed put, wedged into place. Grabbing a screwdriver, Jamie hammered it gently into the top corner and forced the panel loose.

Too nervous to take a look, Abigail held onto the sheet while Jamie tucked his head through the newly created clearing in the wall.

'Is-is there anything there?' she asked.

'Oh, yeah!' Jamie replied. 'And I think you'd better call the police!'

'What?' With curiosity overriding nervousness, she rushed forward, discarding the sheet of MDF without a second thought for where it landed.

Jamie held his torch above her as she stepped into the opening, illuminating the discovery.

Abigail gasped, her hands recoiling to cup her face. Utterly speechless.

'Watch your feet. Some of it might be unstable.'

The floor was strewn with an assortment of bullets and cartridges. Boxes, reminiscent of cigarette packets, were stacked high. Hundreds, if not thousands, of them. Empty shells lay scattered among loose live bullets. Swords, machetes, and bayonets, along with an assortment of daggers, lay criss-crossed among the bullets as if there'd been not a care as to where they'd landed.

Rooted to the spot, Abigail watched Jamie as he crouched down to examine their find.

'Nine-millimetre pistol bullets, shotgun cartridges and .22-calibre rifle bullets. There must be thousands.'

'My grandfather—'

Jamie nodded.

'What's that?' Abigail pointed to a green metal box. It was set apart from everything else, as though it should be avoided, or protected – she couldn't decide which.

Jamie shone his torch. The word *NATO* was plastered across the sides next to what looked to be a serial number.

'I'm not sure we want to be the ones to open that.'

'Why?'

'Well, I'm thinking grenades, but I'm hoping I'm wrong.'

'Grenades!'

'You'd better call the police, unless you want me to do it?'

Abigail took her phone from her pocket but quickly replaced it. 'Can I use yours? My reception's not been so good lately.'

'Yeah, sure,' he replied, handing over his phone.

Given it wasn't exactly an emergency, she dialled 101 and explained their find to the friendly female operator on the other end of the phone.

'It'll be the firearms unit that will come out. They shouldn't be too long,' the operator reassured her before hanging up.

'Here, take this,' Jamie instructed, handing her the torch. 'I'll remove more of the wall, give us more space, and let a bit more light in. But whatever you do, don't touch anything. We've no idea how long this has been here.'

Abigail took the torch and shone it around the newly discovered room. She scolded herself that she'd not thought to wash the outsides of the tiny windows beforehand. That would have let in more natural light.

Their unwelcome discovery covered half of the rear of the house, while the surrounding space was crammed full of what Abigail hoped were clues to her grandmother's past.

Cardboard boxes were piled high and rows deep. An assortment of wicker baskets overflowing with what looked to be clothing was scattered around, along with a few old handbags and a couple of old chests.

'Wow, if you ignore the obvious, it's like an Aladdin's cave up here,' she said, already revelling in the prospect of going through it all, one box at a time, after they'd dealt with the imminent issue, of course.

Jamie appeared to be far more cautious and seemed relieved when the first box Abigail opened was full of old crockery.

'You know, maybe there's nothing to worry about up here, memory-wise,' Abigail suggested, unravelling an old bone china teacup and saucer with dainty red rosebuds from an old tea towel. 'This is gorgeous.'

'Then why not store it in the usable attic space? Why feel the need to hide it away behind a fake wall?'

Abigail thought for a moment. 'Maybe this was a wedding present. Maybe she hid it all to blot out her married years, given how unhappy she must have been with my grandfather?'

'Perhaps.' Jamie looked less convinced.

Abigail had worked her way through the first half dozen boxes by the time the firearms unit arrived. So far, all she'd uncovered was old crockery and kitchenware. She'd found the rest of the rosebud tea set and a selection of old bowls and casserole dishes.

A couple she kept out. They had gone full circle and had come back into fashion and, she decided, would look nice in her kitchen. She was just repacking the box when there was a knock at the door.

Two firearms officers stood on the porch, shoulders back,

chests out. Their bulletproof vests and laden utility belts only added to their bulk, meaning they each filled the doorway as they followed Abigail and Jamie into the attic.

Abigail was aware she and Jamie were doing all the talking, the officers listening as they scanned the surroundings.

Abigail watched as the two men surveyed every inch of the attic before crouching down to examine the find. They methodically lifted and examined one bullet after another, chatting among themselves as to the calibres and sheer volume.

Eventually, they turned their attention back to Abigail and Jamie, asking them questions that reiterated what Abigail had already told the operator on the phone.

After a few minutes, Abigail could see their demeanours changing. The two officers had begun to relax. Probably because they'd been unsure of the situation they'd been walking in to. Abigail took their now chatty manner to mean she and Jamie weren't under suspicion or were no longer seen as a threat.

A little firearm nerdiness came to the fore as the two officers got excited over a box of particularly rare bullets, before confirming Jamie's thoughts as to the 9 mm and .22 calibres.

'Oh, look at this. Your grandfather was a busy man,' the shorter officer announced.

'What do you mean?'

'Well, this is a crimper.' He held up a small metal contraption so Abigail could have a closer look. 'He was making his own bullets up here.'

'What!'

'Yeah,' agreed his associate. 'That's why there are all these empty shells. They were still to be filled. He'd be in a lot of trouble if he were still alive, with the sheer volume, I mean. Was he in the military?'

'No, not that I know of.' Abigail turned to Jamie for confirmation.

He shook his head in agreement.

'And what about that?' the officer asked, nodding towards the NATO box. 'Have you opened it?'

'No,' Jamie replied. 'We didn't, just in case.'

Abigail instinctively took a step back as the shorter officer stood up and stepped through the gruesome assortment to take a closer look.

Cautiously, he lifted the lid. 'Spent machine gun magazines,' he announced to the other officer. 'And some old photos. No grenades.'

The taller officer laughed. 'Well, that makes a pleasant change. Grenades are a common find in these boxes.'

But Abigail was still hung up on the words *spent* and *machine gun*. 'What, *spent*, as in been used? A-a machine gun?'

The shorter officer nodded. 'Yup, and old family photos this time. A much better find!' Smiling, as though he were doing her a favour, giving her memories of family members long-gone, he handed Abigail the bundle.

Abigail glanced down at the first photo, while the officers explained to Jamie that they would arrange for a police van to come and take everything away as soon as possible.

Abigail heard what they were saying, but it didn't register. She was lost in the photo still gracing the top of the bundle.

Jamie stepped in. 'Okay, thank you very much for coming out so quickly. We really appreciate it.'

'Not a problem,' replied the shorter officer. 'The van should be here within the hour. Unfortunately, there's just far too much for us to take it with us.'

And with that, the officers said their goodbyes and Jamie showed them to the door.

When he returned to the attic, Abigail was still standing where he'd left her, still staring at the old photos.

'What's wrong?'

She didn't say a word. Instead, she handed him the photo. He studied the faces of the five men standing in a line, all dressed in camouflage, holding an assortment of rifles and handguns that would have needed the assortment of ammunition currently lying at their feet.

'There, that's him. That's your grandfather.' He pointed to the man second from the left.

Abigail examined his face for a flicker of recognition, but nothing.

'And the man to his right. Do you recognise him?' she asked.

'No, why do you?'

'Yeah, he's the American Tourist!'

'Wh— Are you sure?' He studied the face again. Abigail knew Jamie had only seen the American Tourist the day they'd followed him to the old warehouse, and even then, it'd mostly been from the back.

'I'm one hundred per cent sure! I mean, he's a bit younger

here, not much, but it's one hundred per cent him.'

'It can't be much more than eight years old.'

'How do you know?'

'Because your grandad looks about the same age there as he was when he died.'

'Are you sure?'

'Absolutely.' Jamie nodded. 'I'd put money on it.'

Abigail continued to look through the bundle of photographs. Some were much older, and Abigail was able to spot her grandad in most of them. The same five people were in almost all the photographs, although occasionally another person would appear in the line-up or the background somewhere.

'Jamie, have you noticed'—she began handing him photos one at a time—'my grandfather is always standing beside the American Tourist, in every single one?'

Jamie's eyes flitted from photograph to photograph. 'Abi, that's not all!'

'What do you mean?'

He grabbed the torch and shone it across each photo, discarding them one at a time until he was left with three.

She grabbed one of the photographs and held Jamie's torch over it.

She felt the colour drain from her face. She grabbed the other two, as if searching for confirmation.

'He's younger, but it's him!'

Abigail went cold. Tears flooded her eyes as she bore into the three photographs. She felt Jamie's arm around her.

'I'm sorry, Abi. I'm so sorry.'

Her tears gave way to sobs. Jamie took her in his arms and held her. But as Abigail melted into his arms, the three images were all she could see.

Just like the others, Greg was dressed in full camouflage gear. And, just like the others, he was holding a rifle.

'I think these photos are the most recent, Abi.'

As confusion gave way to anger, Abigail felt the same rage she'd felt when she'd walked in on Darren. She needed to make sense of what she'd discovered. Needed to understand what Greg's relationship had been with her grandfather, and she needed to know why he'd come into her life now.

Pulling herself from Jamie's hold, she began studying the photographs again for clues. Where had they been taken? Why had they been taken? Were they before or after an unsavoury mission? She was lost in trying to unravel her grandfather's world until Jamie brought her back to reality.

'Abi, look!'

She turned to see him on his knees, with the other photos scattered around him in a timeline he'd created, using her grandfather's face as a guide. 'What am I looking at?'

He took one of the photographs from her hands and placed it beside one of the earliest photographs. 'Do you see it?'

Abigail's hands instinctively cupped her face.

'I'm so sorry, Abi. I'm so sorry.'

'It can't be. It just can't!'

'We could be wrong, but the similarity is undeniable.'

Abigail knew. She felt it. The resemblance was too much to ignore. The American Tourist had to be Greg's father!

Perhaps it was the writer in her, but she could visualise the plot. It made sense. But why? Why had Greg come into her life, and what did he want?

Jamie's mobile dragged her from her thoughts. It was the police, confirming that two officers would be there within the hour to remove the ammunition.

Chapter Twenty-Seven

Having watched the police van disappear from sight with their unsavoury find safely inside, Abigail and Jamie decided to wrap up warm and have lunch on the jetty. Abigail had felt a need for the calming views, while the morning's events fully sank in.

It was the time of year when fleeces and raincoats gave way to padded winter jackets as the outerwear of choice for sitting out on the jetty for any length of time. And Jamie and Abigail had theirs zipped to their chins while they watched the ducks bob carefree on the water as it lapped rhythmically against the jetty's legs.

The breeze, travelling down the loch, serenaded them as nature alerted its surroundings to the arrival of winter.

Abigail bit into her sandwich. It was a mishmash of

leftovers, but the addition of relish had taken it to a delicious level.

'Not bad, considering there's never anything in your fridge.' Jamie smiled.

Abigail managed a chuckle but was emotionally drained from their morning. 'What am I going to do, Jamie?'

'I'm not sure, but we need to think this through before you do or say anything to Greg. We also need to work out why he has come into your life. I mean, there's a chance he was part of the group that came the day your grandfather died. And we don't know who else from the photos – apart from him and the American Tourist – is still around.'

'Do you think he's still part of that group? I mean, they were all friends. That's obvious from the photos?'

'I'm guessing that when you're in with a crowd like that, they're never really your friends. I'm betting each one would be as ruthless as the other.'

At that moment, all Abigail wanted to do was scream and shout as she confronted Greg. She wanted to demand answers and make him pay for what they'd all put her grandmother through.

She needed answers. She needed to know if he was here at Lochside six years ago, when her grandfather had been killed and she and her grandmother had been left for dead. Had he stormed into her grandmother's house? Had he shot her grandfather and attacked her grandmother? Had he attacked her?

And at the same time, she was devastated. What had he been thinking as he'd made love to her? As he'd touched her affectionately, as they'd shared their most intimate moments. What had been going through his mind then?

She knew Jamie was right. Greg was not at all what Abigail had thought. If they were right, he'd been playing her all along to get to…? To get to what? She presumed the ammunition. 'What we do know,' she announced cautiously, 'is that his dad's still around, but he's never mentioned him. He told me he came to the island about six years ago and said something about a fresh start. You'd think, if he'd nothing to hide, and if his father was here on the island, he would've mentioned him, maybe even introduced us by now?'

'Did he say where he came from?'

'No, he just said that he came here and got a job with a guy called Mike Scolin, or Keelan, something like that? When I think about it, though, he was quite cagey when I asked.'

'Scanlan?'

'Yeah, that's it. Mike Scanlan.'

'They reckon he was murdered.'

'What?'

'Yeah, pushed from his ladder.'

'How do you know? How do you know he was pushed? Greg said he'd fallen. That it was an accident.'

'A couple of neighbours in their back garden at the time said they heard him arguing with someone. He was on a roof, replacing tiles, when the neighbours heard raised voices. They couldn't make out what was being said, but suddenly everything went quiet, and then when they went out to their car about fifteen minutes later, Mike was lying dead in the drive.

'The police reckoned the ladder was lying at a strange angle. They couldn't quite get the position of the ladder and the position of the body to tie up. The coroner said he died on impact, from a blow to his head, so he couldn't have crawled after he fell. The blood was also localised around his head. There were no smudges to show the body had been moved. They reckon someone had moved the ladder.'

'How do you know all of this?'

'It was big news on the island at the time. Happened not long before I left to join the army. In fact'—he turned to face Abigail—'it must have happened not long after you left.'

Abigail was trying to piece the facts together when her phone rang. She took it from her pocket and, seeing Greg's face illuminated on her screen, she turned it towards Jamie.

'You have to answer it. Just try to act normal.'

'Hi.' She greeted him through gritted teeth. 'Oh, I'm just having lunch on the jetty, but I've been catching up on my writing this morning.' She glanced towards Jamie. 'Joanna's given me an earlier deadline than expected, so I'm going to have to try and get through my word count.'

She fell silent. 'Yes, okay, can I call you? What? Sorry, can you repeat that? Yes, okay, I'll call you tomorrow.'

Relieved, she placed her phone back in her pocket. 'He wants to go for dinner tomorrow night.'

The ex-army side of Jamie was trying to put things into a logical order, trying to think of a strategic plan that would allow them to find out what Greg was up to without putting Abigail in danger.

'Should we call the police?'

'And say what? All we can prove is that he has gone out with you.'

'Greg said he went to work for Mike Scanlan and that he took over his client list after he died. So that means he was probably working for him before he died.'

'The police will have known that at the time. There must have been no evidence linking him to the death.'

'But we also know that his dad had known my grandfather, for years going by the photos. And then there was my strange encounter with him on the train.'

'Yeah, it's all very odd, but it's also just guesswork and presumption for now. Circumstantial.'

Abigail nodded. 'By the way, how come your phone reception is so clear? I'm having trouble with mine and I thought we were on the same network?'

'We are. Why what's wrong?'

'There's a funny static noise. It's almost like a pulse and an annoying hum. I can hardly make out what people are saying sometimes. Also, the battery's not lasting as long.'

Jamie squinted his eyes as he reached across. 'Can I take a look?'

'Sure.' She handed him her phone.

Abigail turned her attention to the water and the bobbing ducks. She was unaware of Jamie calling her phone from his until she heard him leaving a voicemail. 'Hi, it's me. Call me when you get the chance.'

Then he replayed the voicemail he'd just left on loudspeaker. They both listened to the pulsating background noise and Jamie leaned back in his chair. 'Shit.'

'What's wrong?'

'Your phone's been tapped.'

'What? No.' She laughed. 'Don't be daft.'

'I'm telling you, it has!'

'But why? How would you know?'

'I was a mechanic in the army, Abi. It wasn't just vehicles I worked on.'

Abigail sprang to her feet. She paced the jetty, furious as the morning's revelations danced in her head. And frantically trying to make sense of what Jamie was telling her. 'That piece of…' She grabbed her phone to call Greg.

'No, don't.' Jamie took it from her. 'This is our chance to see what he's up to. He has no idea what we've uncovered this morning.'

It was now his turn to pace the jetty. He rubbed his hands together as though it would speed up his thoughts. 'Right, okay, this is what we should do.'

Retaking his seat, he said, 'First of all, we need to buy you a new phone, but I'll get it through the shop. We can't risk him seeing you or me buying one in town, and there needs to be nothing linking it to you. I can get one delivered as shop stock tomorrow.' Jumping to his feet, he started pacing again. 'But we can't let him suspect anything, so we need a reason for us not using your phone.'

Abigail watched on as Jamie hatched his plan.

'You should phone me back. Return my call,' he instructed, handing her back her phone. 'And we can pretend we've fallen out, and that you don't want me calling you again. That way he'll think I'm out of the picture for a bit, which should please him. Then you and I will only call each other using the new phone. Use your old one for any general stuff, though. Don't stop using it altogether. He can't suspect a thing.'

Abigail processed Jamie's words and the morning's events. She couldn't quite believe the twists and turns her life had taken, yet again, in only a few short hours. 'I knew there was a story wrapped around the American Tourist. I just had no idea how close to home it would come.'

Jamie nudged her hand. 'Go ahead, call me. I'll go back up to the house so that he doesn't hear us speaking in the background. But I'm staying here tonight, just in case Greg decides to show up, given our supposed falling out.'

She unlocked her phone and dialled Jamie's number. Her heart pounded in her chest as she waited on him to answer.

'Hey, Abi.'

'Don't *hey* me.' She yelled down the phone. 'I'm too damn angry with you. How could you, Jamie? I thought we were friends?' She gushed. 'Well not anymore. Don't bother calling back. We're done.' Abigail hung up and threw her phone on her cushion, as if it were about to burn her or cause her horrendous pain.

'Well, that came a little too easily. Anything you want to say?' He chuckled, running down the jetty towards her.

Abigail laughed nervously. 'I'm sorry, I needed to shout

at someone. So, what now?'

'Now we wait. See how he reacts to the thought of me being out of the picture. But I think we need to do some digging, see who owns that warehouse your American Tourist went into.'

'Now you're talking,' Abigail enthused. 'And we need to finish searching the attic, see if there are any more clues in among the old boxes.'

Jamie's phone sprang to life, interrupting their plotting. 'Claire,' he said, showing Abigail his screen. 'Bloody hell, she's relentless.'

'Are you going to answer it?'

'Hell, no.'

Chapter Twenty-Eight

Pacing the floor, Greg was aware time was running out. His father, who wasn't the most understanding man at the best of times, was already losing his patience at the length of time the whole operation was taking.

But Greg still hadn't quite mustered up the courage to tell his father about the multiple police visits to Lochside. Greg had often kept an eye on Abigail, from a distance, in the hope she would lead him to the haul his father was so desperate to find.

And yesterday, just like most other days, he'd been sitting in the woods, watching Abigail and Jamie as they sat on the jetty, as she lied to him about her new deadline and the morning she had supposedly spent writing.

He'd seen the firearms police arrive, and he'd seen his father's ammunition carried out in evidence bags and boxes. But there had been no sign of the only incriminating evidence left: the diamonds his father felt were rightfully his. But just because he hadn't seen them, didn't mean the police hadn't found them. All he could do was hope.

Just like the rest of the gang, Greg feared his father. But he also admired him, just as he had admired Abigail's grandfather.

Greg had grown up with the two men at the helm. They'd had a strong bond, like brothers. And it was a bond that no one had managed to break, not even Abigail's grandmother. Until, that is, the day Greg had watched his father shoot Abigail's grandfather in the back.

He'd been devastated. Abigail's grandfather had been like an uncle to him and, unable to show his fear or emotions to his father, he'd had to swallow the pain, burying it deep inside.

At the time, he'd thought about running away, leaving the gang behind, and starting over. But he realised that if his father ever found him, he would go the same way as Abigail's grandfather. He may be his son, but he knew too much. That would make him disposable, even in his father's eyes.

Instead, he'd knuckled down, replacing his father's deceased sidekick as second in command. Together they'd planned and carried out numerous heists. They were set for life. And his father often spoke about retiring to a lavish lifestyle in the depths of the Caribbean or the Far East.

His thoughts turned to Abigail. He was finding her a hindrance. The ammunition was likely all gone, but the diamonds should still be around somewhere, and he was determined to find them.

He'd considered changing tactics with Abigail, getting forceful. But her secrecy around the ammunition meant she was already suspicious, and he was going to have to tread carefully so he didn't end up out of the picture altogether. She was too damn smart for her own good. He'd give it another week, he decided. Schmooze the bitch, wine and dine her, and get her all loved up. Find out what she knew.

His phone buzzed into action.

'Dad.'

'Any news?'

'No, nothing yet. She knows nothing, remembers nothing, and has found nothing. It's like looking for a needle in a haystack.'

'It's taking far too long. You gotta get inventive, understand? I've been on this island far too long already. It's not safe to stick around. You've one week, then I'm stepping in. Understood?' And with that, the line went dead.

He knew what his dad meant by stepping in: a beating until she spoke. But that would get messy, especially with the bloody ex-soldier sniffing around all the time.

He pulled Abigail from his contact list. There were too many rings for his liking before she answered.

Chapter Twenty-Nine

Leaning back in her writing chair, Abigail's gaze drifted, as it often did, across the choppy water. Low angry clouds forming over the mountains in the distance spilled down towards the loch, in a mood that reflected her own.

Heartache, deceit, anger: they'd been Abigail's go-to emotions from the minute Jamie had found the photographs of her grandfather, the American Tourist, and Greg in the attic.

And the only thing stopping her from falling onto the sofa to nurse her second broken heart in less than a year was the feeling that Greg had in some way changed during their most recent conversations. As if he knew what she'd uncovered, or he suspected at least.

She feared time was running out. Greg was obviously not

the gentleman he claimed to be, and there'd been a reason, other than attraction, that'd led him to ensuring he became part of her life. If she and Jamie were to get to the bottom of what was going on, they were going to have to act quickly.

Looking at the diamanté hands, she was frustrated to see it'd only just gone ten. Jamie had returned to the village to cover the shop for his parents for a few hours while they travelled to the wholesalers on the mainland.

With no time to waste, Abigail hurried to the hall cupboard and pulled out a zipped bag that she'd stuffed into its depths months before.

As she threw the contents onto her bed, she was thankful she'd forgotten to take them with her when she'd returned to London for her launch.

Sorting through the hideous theatre ensemble, she picked up the skirt and gave it a shake before doing the same with the jacket. And given she'd been brought up by her grandmother to roll rather than fold, they weren't too badly creased.

The wig was more of a concern, though. Being unsure of what to do with the frizzy mass, she plugged in her curling iron before rushing to the kitchen. She grabbed a mixing bowl and, placing it upside down, she placed the wig on top.

In a town so small, she had to have a convincing disguise. Fortunately, Greg had never seen her in this outfit. Although his father had; the thought jolted her. No, she would be careful. She needed to follow Greg, see what he was up to and where he went.

Changing outfits, she'd forgotten the heftiness of the

padded tweed jacket, as she buttoned up the front and neatened the dated collar.

Once dressed, she attacked the wig with her curling iron. A strange smell engulfed her nostrils as she worked her way around the mass of fake curls.

Leaving them to cool into place, she tied her own hair back into a ponytail before wrapping it around into as flat a bun as she could. Then, after layering on her make-up, not quite as thickly as she'd done for the show, she added the wig and combed the curls out slightly.

Grabbing only her mobile and keys, she rushed to her car and drove to Portree. She parked in the centre; her first port of call was the café.

'Hello. Can I help you?'

Relieved her friend hadn't recognised her, she took a slip of paper from her pocket and handed it to Miranda. 'If I'm not back here in two hours, will you call Jamie and tell him I've gone to the warehouse? He'll know what you mean.'

'What? Sorry, who are y—' Miranda squinted. 'Abigail, is that you?'

'Shh, two hours, then call Jamie,' she reiterated, pointing towards the number scribbled on the piece of paper. 'I'll see you later.'

Approaching the unnamed warehouse nestled in the industrial area on Dunvegan Road, Abigail stepped into a hedgerow. She scanned the surrounding area for any sign of her American Tourist or his deceitful son. But nothing. Unlike the neighbouring mechanics, the car hire company, and the local produce wholesalers, the building looked unwelcoming and abandoned.

They all had their doors flung open, letting the outside world in as they set about repairing cars, selling local produce, and getting on with the day-to-day life that kept the island and its people going.

All were one and a half storeys, and all were much larger on the inside than they'd initially appeared from the hedgerow's depths.

Taking her phone from her pocket, Abigail switched it to silent. She zoomed in on the windows, clicking as she went, hoping that later when she had time to study them, she would find a clue as to what was going on behind the closed doors.

Moments later, she heard a car slowing as it approached the warehouse from Dunvegan Road. Recognising the sound of the engine, she knew instantly it was Greg.

She watched as he parked away from the building, beside a familiar black estate car that looked more used to muddy farm tracks than a town, then he made his way inside.

Frustrated that the windows were so filthy, Abigail edged her way along the hedge that divided the warehouse and a local charity building, to get a closer look. Her heart beat so loud it was echoing in her ears, getting in the way as she tried to listen for any clue as to what was going on inside.

Tucking herself under a small side window, she hunched down and wiped a clear strip along the lower edge of the glass.

Greg was talking, but Abigail was unable to see his companion. Her finger instinctively ran itself further along the murky surface until a woman – in her early thirties, Abigail decided – wandered into view.

Unable to see her face, Abigail watched as the woman wrapped her arms around Greg seductively, as though she'd done so many times before.

The deceit and anger Abigail had felt as she'd watched him approach the warehouse was instantly eradicated, replaced instead by heartache and dejection as she watched them get lost in a passionate embrace that mirrored so many of the moments she'd shared with him.

But their moment of passion was interrupted. Raised voices ensued as the American Tourist came down a set of metal stairs, arms flailing, his rage obvious.

Greg and the woman appeared to endure the verbal onslaught, as if they knew their place, until the American Tourist calmed down.

But whatever had been said had left them flustered. Abigail continued to watch as the woman grabbed her handbag and gave Greg a quick kiss goodbye before leaving the warehouse and running past Abigail towards a small silver car.

But Abigail's hands shot to her face to quieten her gasp. The other woman was Claire. She was sure of it. They'd never met. For some reason Jamie had chosen to keep Claire distant from their friendship – but Abigail was certain. Hers was the face that'd illuminated Jamie's phone screen.

The American Tourist's arms flailed again, his rage reignited as he directed his anger towards Greg. Abigail couldn't make out what was being said, but she'd seen enough.

Chapter Thirty

After waving off another happy customer, Jamie turned his attention back to preparing orders he planned to deliver once his parents had returned from the mainland.

He found the confines of the store frustrating, longing always to be by the water, working on his boats and breathing in the fresh sea air.

The ringing of the bell above the door alerted him to the arrival of customers. 'Good afternoon,' he managed from the depths of the aisles as he gathered up the final order.

'James Campbell?'

'Yes,' he replied, discarding the order, and following the abrupt tones of whoever had found it necessary to use his full name.

But two police officers sent a shiver up his spine as they

turned up the aisle towards him.

'Constables Davis and Sutherland. We are looking for Abigail Sinclair about ammunition found on her property. We believe you were also present when the discovery was made?'

'Yeah, we both were.'

'Do you happen to know where Miss Sinclair is?'

'At her house, I think.'

'We've just come from there. There's no sign of her or her car. Would you know where she might be?'

'No, can you tell me what this is about?'

'The ammunition found on Miss Sinclair's property is linked to several criminal offences still under investigation. Is there anything you or Miss Sinclair aren't sharing with us?'

'No! But if it's linked to criminal offences, that's hardly a surprise given the life her grandfather led. You know about her grandfather, don't you?'

Silence.

'Look, Abigail and her grandmother spent years hiding at Lochside. Abigail's grandmother did all she could to break ties with her husband and managed successfully, too, until he tracked her down.'

'When was that?'

'When Abigail was about eleven. After that, her grandmother lived in fear each time he returned. They both did.'

The burlier officer stayed quiet, scribbling in his notepad while the other asked the questions.

'And Miss Sinclair can back this up?'

'Yes. Well, no, actually. She can't.' Jamie scratched his

head in frustration, realising how unreliable he sounded. 'Not all of it. She can't remember much past her childhood. She has dissociative amnesia, and has done since—' He broke off. 'Wait, you must know about that day. You must know about what happened to her and her grandmother. They'd nothing to do with the find in the attic.'

'I'm afraid we can't discuss that, not with the ongoing investigation. You're sure there was nothing else in the attic. Diamonds, perhaps?'

'Diamonds. No, no, what diamonds? Look, Abigail's not a thief if that's what you're thinking, and neither am I for that matter. Apart from old dishes, clothing, and photos, your men took everything we found on the day.'

'If you see Miss Sinclair, tell her to get in touch.' And with that, they left.

Chapter Thirty-One

'Hi, babe.'

'Claire. What the hell are you doing here?' The police hadn't been gone ten minutes, and he'd enough going on without her hanging around.

'Just come to say hello.' She dropped her voice to a whisper. 'Thought you might like some company while you're stuck in this god-forsaken place.' Jamie watched as she eyed the shop with disgust.

'It's fine. My parents will be back soon and, anyway, we're done.'

'Aww, babe, come on. You know you don't mean that,' she replied, reaching for a kiss.

Jamie managed to dodge her efforts and darted behind the counter, slamming the countertop down to ensure their distance.

'Aww, come on, babe. I'll stick around. Maybe we could go somewhere quiet once you've escaped here.' She walked her fingers across the counter towards his hand.

'Look, Claire, I'm busy. You and I are done. And, anyway, you were never that interested in me when we were going out, so why the sudden interest now?'

But just as the words were escaping his lips, his suspicions were aroused. Suddenly everything was slotting into place.

His mobile rang. *Miranda's* flashed onto his screen. He and Abigail had ordered so many carry-outs that the café was in both their contact lists.

'Oh, babe, ignore it. I'm here.' She flipped the phone from his grasp, harshly enough to confirm his suspicions.

Before he could answer, the shop phone sprang to life. He recognised Miranda's number. After a spring and summer spent covering for his dad when he was having his knee operation, Jamie had gotten to know many local traders' numbers off by heart as they phoned in orders or were desperately in need of ingredients they'd run out of.

Lying to Claire, he said, 'It's Mum. I have to answer.'

Oh, babe, don't be long.'

'Hi, Mum. Yes, I know, go on.'

Jamie listened as Miranda explained that, while it had only been forty minutes, she was too worried about Abigail to wait the full two hours.

He needed to get rid of Claire and quickly. 'Okay, Mum. Thanks.'

Doing his best to sound convincing, he said, 'They're

almost back. Just a few minutes away.' And knowing she would never want to hang around and meet them, he added, 'Why don't you go and wait for me on the bench by the road end. We could go for a walk along the coast. I'll join you as soon as they get back.'

'Really.' She blurted, almost falling out of character in shock.

'Yeah, maybe we should talk. Maybe I was too hasty.'

Cringing, he allowed her to kiss him before she slunk out of the shop in an outfit more suited to someone fifteen years her junior.

Waiting until she'd disappeared out of sight, Jamie flipped the shop sign to *Closed*, locked up, and ran out of the back door to his truck. Driving in the opposite direction, he headed to Portree and the warehouse.

Chapter Thirty-Two

Greg may have been a criminal, but he was also the second person to string Abigail along in recent time. And the realisation that Greg had never loved her. That she'd been fooled again. That his words, his touch, and his passion were all a ruse to find her grandfather's hoard: this all amplified the pain and heartache she'd felt with Darren.

Wiping at tears, she made her way through the quiet streets towards her car. It was a quieter time of year on the island and the colder weather meant most tourists were either in somewhere savouring a tasty meal or were back in their hotels enjoying a drink and an open fire. The hardier ones would still be in the hills, walking the Quiraing or up to the Old Man of Storr.

She'd no idea how she was going to tell Jamie that Claire

was involved. She couldn't bear the thought of him feeling as used, exploited, or as dispensable as she did.

Approaching her car, Abigail fumbled for her keys. She searched the pockets of the old tweed jacket. The pocket linings had become worn, frayed, and ripped in places, alluding to its many ventures on stage.

Frustrated at the jingle she couldn't quite locate, she eventually felt the cold metal brush against her fingers.

And just as she wrapped her fingers around the key, a hand grabbed her from behind, clasping her mouth, stopping her from releasing a scream that was desperately crying out from within.

Another hand clasped her waist and pulled her backwards. Her feet grappled to find solid ground as her abductor kept her off balance. Her hands desperately pulled at the stranger, clawing at his clothes, grabbing at his hands but to no avail.

She bit his hand and tried again to scream, to kick out. But while his hand covered her mouth, it also rested against her nostrils.

Unable to breathe, she was quickly overpowered. Her assailant rammed her into the back of a car with its engine running. They sped off. The stranger's hands held her down, the weight of his body holding her firmly in place.

Abigail recognised the driver. It may have been from behind, but she knew it was her American Tourist. It wouldn't be long before they realised she was wearing a wig and discovered her true identity.

Abigail knew she couldn't allow that to happen. She had to fight back. She had to gather her senses and take charge. Easier said than done as she tried to control her shaking.

But her fear was now marred with anger. Although she was unable to see the street outside, she spotted the church steeple, meaning they were still near the centre of town. Her assailants didn't seem to be taking her far.

The car slowed to a halt. Going by the position of the steeple, Abigail thought maybe they'd stopped at the pedestrian crossing just around the corner from the town square. And, although it was December, she knew tourist season was year-round on the island. There were bound to be a few people wandering around. This was her chance.

While her assailant's hands still clasped her mouth, his body weighing hers down, her legs trapped beneath him, she let her body go limp. And pulling her limp arm back, Abigail clenched her fist and thrust it downwards, punching her abductor as hard as she could between his legs. She took a look at his face.

He recoiled, released his grip, and bent double, groaning in pain. Abigail grappled for the door handle and fell out of the car just as it started to move off. Her legs were still trapped under her assailant's body, and her shoulder dragged along the tarmac.

He pulled at her. Grasping at her clothes, her legs, anything, he tried to get enough of a grip to haul her back into the car. His hands grabbed at her body, his fingers bearing deep into the fleshy tissue of her limbs.

Knowing she had to fight through the pain, she tugged her legs, kicking them upwards until her right leg finally broke free. With an almighty kick, she caught him square in the face.

Eyes, evil and cold, bore down on her. Eyes that'd lured her in with passion and wanting. Eyes that'd fooled her. Eyes that'd enveloped her body in the throes of passion. Eyes that'd cared for her, loved her, and laughed with her.

The driver increased his speed. She pulled at her trapped leg while still kicking with the other. The pain from her shoulder was excruciating, now through to raw flesh. Her head pounding, she tried to keep it from bouncing off the tarmac. Gravel was thrown into her eyes and mouth from the moving tyres.

Her head bounced off the tarmac again, the pain searing through her neck and down her spine into her back. She could feel her eyes close, feel herself lose consciousness, until screams from pedestrians alerted her to the fact she wasn't alone.

Finding the strength for one last almighty kick, Abigail freed her trapped leg and slumped onto the road as the car sped off.

As people gathered, the pain in her head from the final thud as she'd landed was all-consuming. And, as they crouched around her, asking if she knew her name or knew where she was, her surroundings went quiet. Her eyes closed.

Chapter Thirty-Three

As Jamie ran down the corridor towards Abigail's bedside, the overwhelming dread and panic he'd felt six years before was engulfing him once again.

With a reputation for dealing with serious trauma from mountaineering accidents, Broadford Hospital had been chosen for Abigail's initial assessment.

'Abigail Sinclair,' he begged, catching his breath.

'She's being assessed just now, sir. Are you family?'

'Yeah, well, no. But I'm the closest thing to family she's got.'

'I'm sorry, sir, I can't tell you anything.'

'But I'm all she's got. Is she going to be okay? Can I see her?'

'She's currently being assessed. Take a seat. I'll see if a

doctor will speak to you once they're finished. That's the best I can do.'

Jamie slumped into the chair nearest the desk, racking his brains, blaming himself for not trying to do more to find out what Greg and his father were up to. The army had trained him to be methodical and never to enter battle without a plan.

Abigail, on the other hand, was headstrong and independent. He was cursing her for not waiting for him. But at the same time, knowing her as he did, he wouldn't have expected anything else.

Minutes turned into a couple of hours before a familiar face finally walked through the doors towards him.

'I believe you're here for Miss Sinclair?'

'Yes, how is—'

'Ahh, you were the fiancé.'

Jamie nodded.

'I'm Doctor Macpherson. It was me who spoke to you six years ago. I remember you and Abigail. Some cases stay with you, and you had all been through so much.'

Jamie nodded. 'Yes, that's me.' He knew if he played along, the doctor would be able to open up about how she was.

'Well, she's sleeping just now. But *lucky* is how I would describe her. Very lucky indeed. It could have been much worse.'

'Go on,' Jamie pleaded.

'Well, fortunately, there were witnesses, and the paramedics were able to paint a decent picture of what happened. I have to say, if the car had been able to go any faster, things would probably have ended differently. But some of the witnesses did a

226

good job of blocking the car and slowing it down. Meaning that, while serious, the bumps to the head are not life-threatening.

'She had a dislocated shoulder. We've popped it back into place and dressed her flesh wounds. They're all strapped up, although we will be keeping an eye on them. We've done X-rays. There are no broken bones, but there are plenty of bruises showing already, mainly on her hips, back, and shoulders. Some around her ankles and lower legs, consistent with a struggle. There will be plenty more bruises to come out over the next few days too. And, with them, various other aches and pains, especially in her back and neck.

'We've given her something for the pain and to make her sleep. Rest is crucial just now, but she'll be able to stay here. She won't need to be transferred to the mainland.'

Jamie slumped into his chair. With his elbows on his knees, he held his head in his hands. The doctor sat beside him.

'She's going to be okay. Obviously, a serious incident has taken place, and we have notified the police of her condition. And we will let them know when she wakes.'

Jamie nodded. 'Of course. I'm going to talk to them myself. Unfortunately, this is linked to what happened six years ago. We need to put a stop to it once and for all.'

The doctor stayed quiet.

'Can I see her?'

'Just for a minute. But first, just before we gave Abigail something to help her sleep, she was talking. Able to tell us how she was feeling, answering questions. And I gather her memories had never returned?'

Jamie shook his head.

'With her leaving the island so abruptly, we were never able to oversee her care. We had hoped she would've registered with a doctor elsewhere, but it doesn't appear that she did. Anyway, that's by the by now. But as she was dozing off, she seemed to flinch, and muttered something about remembering. Then the medication kicked in and she fell asleep.'

'What? You mean remembering her lost years?'

Doctor Macpherson shrugged. 'We won't know that until she wakes. But, with that in mind, we will be keeping her sedated until we are sure she is out of severe pain. If her memories have returned, she will have enough to deal with when she wakes.'

Nodding, Jamie said, 'Can I see her now?'

'Of course. This way.'

Jamie followed him through to the same unit Abigail had been admitted to six years before.

Bandages encased her head. Grazes, scratches, bruises covered her face. And from under the sheets, bandages stretched from her torso across both her shoulders.

Tears flooded Jamie's eyes, running down his cheeks, as he took her hand. Crouching beside her, he said, 'Abi, it's Jamie. I'm here.' His fingers travelled gently across her bruised fingers. 'I'm here, and I love you. Whatever you remember, just know I love you.'

'Okay, that's time.'

Jamie gave Doctor Macpherson a quick nod before returning his attention to Abigail. Kissing her gently on the cheek, he told her he would be back soon with some of her belongings.

Did she hear him? He had no idea. Did she know how he truly felt? He had no idea.

'Thank you, doctor. I'll come back later and sit in reception if that's okay? I just want to be here, in case she wakes.'

The doctor nodded. 'One of the nurses will show you where you can wait. There will be a degree of caution, given the circumstances in which she arrived. You do understand our duty is to Abigail?'

'Of course.'

'When it comes to visitors, I will have to consider the information given to us by the police. Just now, things are still a bit hazy.'

'I understand. I'm heading there now.'

Chapter Thirty-Four

Exasperated, Jamie drove down the dirt track towards Lochside. Having spent an hour at the police station, he felt no further forward now than he had when he'd first arrived.

He understood them needing clarification from Abigail. It was only right she corroborate his version of events. But, having told them everything he and Abigail had uncovered, they didn't yet feel they had enough evidence to find and question Greg. All Jamie could do was hope that they were keeping their cards close to their chests, and that they were, in fact, going to question him.

Daylight had long faded and, as Jamie turned the final corner to Lochside, his headlights caught the choppy waters, glistening over the white horses as they crashed into shore.

A flicker of movement in front of the house caught his eye.

Recognising Greg's puffer jacket, Jamie flicked his headlights off and shut down the engine.

It was hard to make out what was going on in the encroaching darkness, but Greg flicking a torch on allowed Jamie to see him locking the door behind him and walking off into the sparse woodland.

Jumping from his truck, Jamie followed the torchlight. A task made all the harder as the light flickered in and out of sight as Greg made his way through the trees and upwards towards the rolling hills.

As Jamie finally caught up, he could see the path Greg had taken was well worn. It wasn't a route he or Abigail had ever taken, not even when they were younger, so Jamie's guess was that Greg had been a regular on the path.

The torchlight disappeared. Jamie stood still, listening in the cold night air. But the waves, the branches swooshing in the breeze, the hoot from the owls combined to drown out any noise that Greg might make.

Peering through the darkness at where he'd last seen the light, Jamie caught a glimpse of a shack. It was crudely built, and barely big enough for a child. But a lifetime on the island meant Jamie knew this was no wildlife hide.

As he crept closer, something snapped underfoot. Jamie stayed rooted to the spot, barely breathing, in the hope Greg would think it was a pine marten or a fox.

Trying to get his bearings, Jamie decided they must be near the old track that led from the main road to the abandoned Thomson farm. It meandered parallel to the one that led to

Lochside before eventually snaking off into the hills.

It was all falling into place. That sneaky bastard. He'd been keeping watch. Jamie thought back to his and Abigail's fake fall out over her tapped mobile phone.

Greg had known all along they were together. He'd been watching. Shit. Jamie realised he must also have known about their find in the attic. He'd have seen it being driven off. So why were they still here? What else were they looking for?

Diamonds. He remembered one of the policemen mentioned something about diamonds when they came into the shop looking for Abigail.

The pieces may have been falling into place, but Jamie knew it was far from over. If diamonds were what Greg and his father were after, and they suspected they were still at Lochside, then Abigail still wasn't safe. He needed to speak to the police again, and he needed to warn Doctor Macpherson.

Retracing his steps, Jamie headed back towards his truck. He could only presume that Greg and his father were hiding out at the old farm and that would hopefully keep Greg out of the way for now.

Approaching his truck, Jamie heard a shuffle in the trees. Greg's father. He lunged towards him, wielding a plank of wood. Jamie braced and threw a punch, connecting with his attacker's chin, sending him hurtling to the ground. But not before he felt a thud on the side of his head, and all went dark.

Chapter Thirty-Five

'Abigail, Abi, it's okay, honey. You can open your eyes if you're feeling up to it.'

Abigail's eyes continued to twitch and flutter until both the hospital room and Morag came into focus.

'It's alright, dear. How are you feeling?'

She looked around the room. 'Where's...' Her mouth was dry. Her face and head ached and more so when she spoke. 'Where's Jamie?'

'He'll be here. Don't worry. He-he's just helping the police with their enquiries. I've buzzed so the doctor will be in to see you in a minute.'

With that, the doctor wandered in, clipboard in hand. 'Good morning, Abigail. How are you feeling?'

Abigail's head was foggy. She struggled to piece together

the events that'd led to her being in so much pain.

Morag, apparently sensing her confusion, reached for her hand and held it tightly while the doctor shone a light into her eyes, took her pulse, and checked the various monitors beeping and flashing at her bedside.

Abigail recognised Morag, but the first thing that struck her was how she'd aged. 'Is-is the shop okay? I mean, is it okay that you're here?'

'Oh, good grief, don't you go worrying about the shop. There was no way I was having you waking up on your own. Today is a good day. Doctor Macpherson has reduced your medication.'

Doctor Macpherson, a trainee doctor, and a couple of nurses set about assessing Abigail. Morag stepped out to give them their privacy and sneaked along the corridor to make a phone call.

'Any news?'

'Nothing yet, dear. I'm sorry. His truck's been checked by forensics. It's been well and truly trashed. The police are arranging to have it towed. They'll keep it just now. Although, to be honest, after I've taken his belongings out, it's in no fit state to be given back.'

'Is there any clue as to what's happened? Anything?' Morag sobbed.

'There are signs of a scuffle. Fortunately, because there's been rain over the last few days, the ground was wet, and the police have identified Jamie's footprints and one other set. They've managed to match Jamie's to a partial gravel print in the footwell of his truck. They can tell there's been a bit of a struggle because of the way the footprints have smudged. Jamie has probably braced his right leg to either swing a punch or block someone else's.'

Morag's sobs continued as she listened to her husband's update. 'What are the police going to do now? Are they looking for him?'

'Yes, they've managed to collect some fibres and, oh, oh, just a minute, dear—'

Morag could hear muffled voices in the background. Her heart pounding, she was dreading what her husband was about to tell her.

'Morag, Morag, they've picked up his footprints. They think he's gone off into the woods by the house and then come back down to the truck. Another set of footprints has been picked up, coming off the porch at the front door and then into the woods, possibly in front of Jamie. I'm going with them. Okay, love? I'll call you as soon as I hear anything.'

Morag patted her eyes and cheeks with a tissue, trying desperately to calm herself before going back in to see Abigail. Doctor Macpherson met her as he came out.

'Any news?'

Morag filled him in. Beginning to sob again, she said, 'I just don't know what to tell Abigail.'

'Tell her nothing. The less she knows, the better at this stage.'

Morag nodded.

'She, eh, she has regained some of her memories. And, as

is common, she's quite upset. Confused as she tries to work out what's reality and what might have been a dream. She's asking for Jamie. She's realising just how close they were and obviously, things have been different since she's returned. I've told her he's still helping the police. Until we know what's happened for sure, that's all she needs to hear at this stage. There's a nurse with her just now.'

As anxious as Morag was about Jamie, she agreed with him.

'She'll have questions. Answer them as gently and as honestly as you can.' Doctor Macpherson gave Morag a gentle pat on the arm and continued up the corridor. 'Oh, by the way, under the circumstances, we are going to monitor visitors. Only you, your husband, and the police are allowed in at the moment. Oh, and Jamie, obviously.'

Stepping through the door, Morag took a deep breath as she prepared herself for whatever questioning was about to follow. 'Hello, dear. How are you doing? Can I get you anything?'

Abigail shook her head. 'Just Jamie. I need to speak to Jamie.'

'I know, dear. The police are needing him just now, or believe you me, he would be here.' Bracing herself, she took Abigail's hand in hers. 'Doctor Macpherson said some of your memories have returned.'

Abigail began to cry.

'Oh no, dear. Try not to cry. That won't help your pounding head.' She took a tissue from her purse and patted Abigail's eyes and cheeks.

'There you are, dear.' Still clutching Abigail's hand, Morag took a seat in the chair beside her bed. 'Your grandmother and I had a pact, you know.'

Abigail winced as she turned her head slightly to face Morag.

'We promised each other that, if anything ever happened to one of us, she would look out for Jamie, and I would look out for you.'

Tears welled in Abigail's eyes. She felt as though she were losing her grandmother all over again. 'I remember. I remember them breaking down the door and my grandmother – she'd been washing dishes – she ran into the hall to see what the commotion was. But they chased her back to the kitchen. She kept trying to get past them, to get back to me. Greg's father threw her to the floor, and she was out cold.'

Morag, still holding Abigail's hand with one hand, blotted her tears with the other.

'My grandfather,' Abigail continued, 'said nothing, but he'd obviously seen them coming down the track as he'd already run out of the back door.' Her face ached, as she sobbed at the betrayal, the deceit, the undeniable lack of love or concern by a grandfather for a granddaughter and his wife. Fighting through her sobs, she said, 'Greg's father, he-he, went after him.'

'Shush, shush, it's okay.' Morag tried to calm Abigail as she became more distressed. 'You don't have to talk about this now, not if you don't want to.'

'I-I need to— We need to tell the police. We need to let

them know. Jamie might be in danger. Greg, it was Greg who attacked me six years ago.'

'And in the car, a couple of days ago, who abducted you? Can you remember?'

'Greg's father was driving.'

'And the other man?'

Abigail turned away. She couldn't face Morag; she couldn't face anyone. And as tears soaked her cheeks, the pain and heartache from a lifetime of abandonment, loss, love, and heartache was all-consuming.

'Was it Greg, dear? We need to let the police know. If you know who it was, we need to tell them.'

But the words were too painful to utter. Abigail tightened her grip on Morag's hand. Morag had engulfed her memories. The woman who'd been a stranger just a few short months ago had, in fact, been an integral part of her life. An integral part of a life far more fulfilling, far more rewarding than she'd remembered.

Wincing in pain, Abigail was unable to stop her tears. Betrayal had overwhelmingly taken hold. Years wasted, believing her grandmother had kept her isolated and alone, had suddenly been flooded with memories of laughter, tranquillity, and peace.

Abigail might not have gone to school. She might not have ventured far from Lochside. But she'd been loved. She'd been cared for, and she'd had Jamie and his parents who welcomed her into their family as one of their own.

Jamie had given her a life full of adventure and fun. He'd

introduced her to hiking, walking, and sailing. Barbecues, picnics, and movie nights.

But she could also remember the times when her grandfather would return. The fear her grandmother had felt while she endured his presence. And the relief they'd all felt when he'd had enough of hiding out. When they would awaken to find him gone.

Turning to Morag, she confirmed, 'Yes, that was Greg too.'

Chapter Thirty-Six

Trepidation choked John Campbell's throat as he followed the police into the woods. Having joined the search for Abigail's grandfather six years ago, he was more than aware of what these people were capable of and what they might find.

He'd only been a few steps behind the officers when they'd made their gruesome discovery, and the image of Abigail's grandfather lying slumped over a fallen branch was still as clear to him today as it was then.

John knew that Mark MacLaren would also be more than aware of how he was feeling. Having gone to school together, John and Sergeant MacLaren had remained good friends. Their families socialised, had even been on holiday together. Their wives were best friends.

He'd know that a gruesome discovery today would hit

unbearably close to home.

'Are you sure we're going in the right direction?' John asked.

'Trust me, the men know what they're doing. The trail leads this way. We've been lucky with the weather. Just keep close behind my men. That way, the footprints are left untouched.'

John did as his friend told him and ventured further upwards through the trees towards the old road. Occasionally a sheep would thrust a bleat in their direction as it scarpered across the wild landscape. But other than that, there had been no sign of anything unusual.

Continuing upwards, he struggled to get his bearings. It'd been years since he'd last ventured this far up the hill. Remembering the old dirt track that led to the abandoned Thomson farm, he presumed they would at some point meet it.

And just as he tried to visualise the geographical landscape, the leading officer held up a hand. Everyone stopped.

Keeping his hand up, the lead officer pointed towards a shack. The two officers behind quickly went to investigate.

'All clear,' signalled one officer while the other crouched onto his knees and shone a torch inside.

Empty drink cans, crisp packets, and cigarette butts lay scattered alongside a couple of blankets and a pair of binoculars.

Turning to look at the views behind, Sergeant MacLaren pointed towards Lochside. 'They've had a clear view of the house from here, John, and the jetty. They'll have seen her coming and going. Known exactly what she's been up to.' Changing his tone, he said, 'It's more than likely they've also got Jamie, or eh'—he faltered—'know where he is.'

John couldn't answer. He felt sick to his core.

'I'm wondering about the old farm,' Sergeant MacLaren added. 'I'll radio in. Get some men up there pronto to take a look around.'

John nodded before following the men further up the hill and into the unknown.

Sergeant MacLaren was proven right when they reached the end of the path. John saw a wire fence was all that separated them from the dirt track leading to the old farm.

Sergeant MacLaren called his men back. 'We can't go any further, not on foot. It's too open. We'll be sitting ducks.'

Taking cover, all they could do was wait.

John's heart pounded. Jamie was their world. Apart from when Jamie had gone off to the army, all three of them – John, Morag, and Jamie – had lived their entire lives on the island. He knew it and its people well.

Islanders were often the kindest, friendliest, most caring of people. Everyone knew everyone, and they were there, without a moment's hesitation, on the days you needed them.

Today was one of those days. He needed Sergeant MacLaren and his men to be there for him today.

'My men are five minutes out. The final vehicle will stop and pick you up, John.'

He noticed a shift in his friend's demeanour. 'Mark? What are you not telling me?'

'You'll need to stay in the car, John. I can't let a civilian walk into this unprepared.'

There were a few minutes of John pleading his case, but it was futile. And the sound of engines saw Sergeant MacLaren's men whip into position as four vehicles approached.

'I'm sorry, but I mean it. You stay put in the car. We think we've established the identities of the two men and'—he lowered his head—'we've brought in the armed officers.'

As Sergeant MacLaren jumped into the lead car, John did as he was instructed and, heart racing, he jumped into the back of the rear car. Recognising both officers in front, he knew his friend had brought out his A-team.

And as they approached the cusp of the hill leading to the farm, John wondered if the team his friend had encircled them with was coincidental or intentional. Did he know more than he was letting on?

Chapter Thirty-Seven

'Can Morag stay?' Abigail pleaded with the two officers who'd arrived to interview her.

Constable Davis nodded while Constable Sutherland placed two extra chairs beside her bed.

Turning to face them, Abigail tightened her grip on Morag's hand. 'Have you found Greg? You need to warn Jamie, Claire's in on it too.'

The officers stayed quiet. 'Miss Sinclair, the day you found the ammunition in the loft, did you find anything else?'

Abigail strained; talking hurt her jaw. 'There was just lots of old stuff. Tea sets, clothes, old photos.' Becoming flustered, she tried to lift her head. Morag pleaded with her to stay calm.

'The old photos. My grandfather was with the guy I'd

nicknamed the American Tourist, and Greg. They were dressed in camouflage and were all holding guns. Jamie and I think the American Tourist is Greg's dad. The similarities are uncanny.'

'Yes, we know. Jamie gave us the same information.' The officer scribbled in his notepad.

The other was taking a photograph from a file he'd been clutching since he arrived. 'Can you identify this man, Miss Sinclair?'

'That's the American Tourist.'

'Was he driving the car? The day you were abducted?'

Nodding, Abigail managed to croak 'Yes.'

The officers ran through their other questions, but the identity of the American Tourist seemed to be the most important thing on their minds.

And Abigail managed a 'Thank you' as they wished her well and went on their way.

She turned her attention to Morag. 'Are you okay? You look pale?'

'Oh, my goodness, girl. You are asking me if I am alright. I'm fine. Now, how about you? How are you feeling? Can I get you anything?'

Abigail shook her head. 'I'm just sore,' she replied, managing a light chuckle. 'But what else can I expect? Just look at the colour of me. I'm like a rainbow.'

Morag leaned in and gave her a gentle hug. 'Now, there's the Abigail I remember.'

'I'm so sorry I had forgotten you.' Tears leaked from Abigail's eyes, dampening the bandages swaddling her head.

'Good grief. Don't you ever apologise for your memory. Ever. Do you hear me?'

'I have so many questions. I'm scared they're not memories. That I made them up, or-or dreamed them.'

'Well, run some by me. Let's sort out what we can together.'

Abigail and Morag sifted through the years, laughing, joking, crying. Remembering the sad times, wishing Abigail's grandmother was here, and laughing at all the happy memories the two families had enjoyed while Abigail and Jamie were growing up.

Half an hour turned into an hour and an hour turned into two. Glad of the distraction, Morag was happy to delve into whatever particular memory Abigail plucked from their past.

But at just gone six, every fibre of her body shuddered as her mobile rang, her husband's smile illuminating the phone as the ringing persisted.

'It's okay. Go answer it,' Abigail instructed. 'I'll be fine.'

Morag walked into the corridor, closing Abigail's door firmly behind her. She'd realised from the police officer's questioning that things were far more serious than she'd known. And now, if she ignored the ring, all could still be fine. After all, no news is good news.

But she couldn't ignore it forever. At some point, reality would have to be faced. And after two days, she was feeling that the reality she craved was slipping ever further from her grasp.

Her finger swiped *Answer*.

'Hello, hello, dear. Are you there?'

Silence. Morag's words choked in her throat.

'Morag, are you there? We've got him. He's okay.'

Morag fell into a chair, missing it slightly, so it bashed off the wall, making a clatter that alerted a nurse.

The nurse came running, helping Morag into her seat in time for tears of sheer relief to pour.

Morag held the phone to her ear, holding the nurse's supporting hand as the fear of losing her son dissipated into the ether.

'He's okay. Morag, he's okay. A bit bruised, but he'd stayed calm, convinced them he knew where the diamonds were, and that they needed him. Smart boy, our Jamie. We are on our way to the hospital now. Jamie needs a check over, a few cuts cleaned, but he's insisting on seeing Abigail first. Is she up to seeing him in this state?'

'Well, they'll be a matching pair.'

Chapter Thirty-Eight

In the days and weeks that followed, Abigail's memories were fully restored. And with them, her sense of humour, her personality, her zest for life.

Getting to know herself all over again had initially felt frightening. But each memory had been intermingled with love and a bond that connected her ever-stronger to her grandmother, Jamie, and his family.

Jamie had taken her to see *their* cottage. She'd encouraged him to decorate it and make it his own. And although she knew he was struggling, she'd kept encouraging.

Like Abigail, he'd lived in limbo for far too long. She knew they both needed to recover, to find their own identities, and to find their way in the world again. Whether that would lead them to each other, only time would tell.

Miranda disturbed her thoughts with a cappuccino and the daily special: a vanilla slice. Abigail was just licking the last of the cream from her fingers when Jamie stuck his head around the café door.

'Sergeant MacLaren's wondering if you have a minute. He's needing a word.'

'What about?'

'Some new information's come to light. Wants to talk to us both.'

Abigail stepped into Sergeant MacLaren's office and took a seat. Jamie sat down beside her. Numerous empty coffee cups were strewn across the desk, as was a paperwork system that she was sure was only known to MacLaren himself. Although, she did have to admit that whatever system he used, it worked. His reputation came before him, and it'd been true to form throughout the days that Jamie had been missing.

He'd also tidied the case up quickly once he'd arrested Greg, his father, and Claire.

'Right, you two. Thought I'd better fill you in now that I'm allowed. Let you both tie up the loose ends and answer the questions you've been asking me over the last few weeks.' He winked at Abigail.

Abigail sat forward, waiting patiently, willing him on.

'Your American Tourist is one Simon Mathieson, wanted for various crimes across Europe and America. Now, eh, this next bit will be unsettling for you, Abigail.'

Abigail was unsure how anything he had to say could be

more unsettling than what she'd already been through.

'Simon Mathieson had been watching you from a distance for years, waiting on you to lead him to diamonds stolen during a heist in Naples, Italy, about a year before he turned up at the house and shot your grandfather.

'Your grandfather had been involved in the heist – one of the main organisers – and Simon Mathieson believed, or, I should say, still believes that your grandfather didn't hand over all the diamonds he'd taken that night, which in turn got your American Tourist into hot water with his boss. Incidentally, the diamonds haven't yet been recovered. So that part of the case is still ongoing.

'But it turns out your American Tourist answers to one Emiliano Romano, who bears a startling resemblance to the man you described from the train when you travelled back here in April.'

'I knew it,' Abigail exclaimed. 'Have you got him?'

'Yes, some of our colleagues on the mainland brought him in this morning. But there's more.'

'More,' Abigail exclaimed, her next book currently writing itself.

'Simon Mathieson knew Darren was cheating on you.'

Abigail flushed. Surely this was information Sergeant MacLaren didn't need to know.

'He'd tailed him, the day you caught him with'—Sergeant MacLaren shuffled uneasily in his seat—'well, the day you caught him with the other woman.

'He threatened him. He knew that his affair had been

going on for about a year.'

Right, okay, rub it in, Abigail thought to herself, willing the conversation to move on.

'He told him to get caught, and pronto, and to abandon your belongings on the landing.'

'How do you know?'

'We've spoken to Darren. He's corroborated Simon's version of events.'

'So, Greg's father has just opened up to you? Given all this information? Just like that?'

'Yeah, well, the idiot's trying to get himself a deal. But he's going down, and he's going down for a long time. But you've been lucky. If the train hadn't been so crowded, he was for whipping you there and then.'

'What? But he didn't know it was me? I was in that old theatre costume.'

'Yes, he did. He'd followed you. He sat in the damn audience the day of your shows. He didn't let you out of his sight.'

Chapter Thirty-Nine

As the sun set over the glistening water, Jamie filled Abigail's thoughts. He'd been patient, hadn't pushed, and had told Abigail often that he had no expectations, that she'd been through enough.

And she had, but now, apart from the missing diamonds, the case was closed. Simon and Greg Mathieson were serving time for multiple armed robberies, kidnapping, attempted murder, and murder. Claire, whose real name turned out to be Jill Bennet, was currently serving a lesser sentence for aiding and abetting.

Emiliano Romano, who'd run his criminal operations from a small town just outside Naples, was also serving time, along with a few of his men. Once Simon Mathieson had been arrested, the net had quickly spread, and Sergeant MacLaren had found himself working an international case alongside police forces across Europe.

But now, Abigail knew it was time to put the past firmly in the past. She couldn't continue to let Simon Mathieson, Greg, or her grandfather determine the path of her own life. Her destiny was hers to make, and hers alone.

Stepping onto the jetty, she ventured out over the cold North Atlantic, the crashing waves shaking the wooden structure beneath her feet. She couldn't help but wonder how her grandmother's rickety old jetty would've fared in such weather.

A storm was rolling in and, although the cold night air enveloped her, caressing her goosebumps as the chill penetrated her many layers, she was rooted to the spot.

Thankful for every memory, every minute she'd spent with her grandmother, and every day she'd spent at Lochside.

'I wouldn't stand there if I were you. It's not looking too safe.'

Jamie walked towards her, a glass of wine in each hand, his eyes wrinkling in the corners as they always did when he looked at her with that smile.

He was strong, reliable. She felt safe in his company. But even more so, she felt alive. And, watching him as he approached her, getting closer, she knew: now it was their turn.

'Maybe we should take this to the porch. It's getting stormy out here.'

Taking her glass, she followed, her hand slipping into his, their silence whispering a thousand sweet nothings as they turned to watch the sunset from the porch.

'Dinner will be ready about seven,' she announced, sipping her wine.

'What time is it now?'

'I'm not sure. I'll check the diamanté hands.'

'Why do you always call your watch the *diamanté hands*? The hands are metal.'

'I don't know. It's what my grandmother always called it.'

Something seemed to dawn on them both at the same time. Suddenly, the glasses were abandoned as they ran to the kitchen.

As Jamie gently prised the back from the watch her grandmother had worn until the day she died, Abigail could only wonder. How many diamonds were about to tumble onto her kitchen table? How many diamonds had adorned her wrist in the last seven years?

If you enjoyed this book…

- Please rate or review *Abigail Returns* on your favourite site.
- Tell your friends.
- Add it to a genre list on Goodreads.
- Share a direct 'buy' link on your social media.
- Connect with the author on social media.
- Visit www.paulinetait.com to sign up for news and events.

Authors work hard to be noticed in the crowded world of books, and often it's word-of-mouth that makes all the difference.

Thank you for your support and help.

Ingram Content Group UK Ltd.
Milton Keynes UK
UKHW011839280423
420960UK00002B/8